Golden Treasury

THIS IS A PARRAGON BOOK

© Parragon 1996
Reprinted 1998

Published by
Parragon
13 Whiteladies Road, Clifton, Bristol BS8 1PB

Produced by
The Templar Company plc,
Pippbrook Mill, London Road, Dorking,
Surrey RH4 1JE

Designed by Mark Kingsley-Monks

Illustrated by:
Stephen Holmes, Jo Caine, David Anstey,
Nigel McMullen, Jenny Press,
Martin Aitchinson, Maggie Downer

Printed in Italy

Hardback ISBN 0 75252 819 X
Paperback ISBN 0 75252 611 1

Golden Treasury

PARRAGON

CONTENTS

INTRODUCTION

Golden Treasury is a collection of classic tales which have been thoughtfully rewritten for a whole new generation of children. The thrill and excitement of adventure stories and fairytales has always captivated the imagination of children and this beautifully illustrated collection is certain to become a firm favourite with children everywhere, to return to again and again.

This volume brings together a selection of the very best tales from around the world. Here are seven stories of Brer Rabbit and his friends, which were first told by Uncle Remus over one hundred years ago and a shortened version of Kenneth Graeme's masterpiece, "The Wind in the Willows". Six of Rudyard Kipling's famous Just-So Stories are also included and five of the most classic nursery tales.

TALES OF BRER RABBIT

Illustrated by Stephen Holmes

STORIES INCLUDED IN
TALES OF BRER RABBIT:

BRER RABBIT AND THE BRAMBLE PATCH
∞
BRER RABBIT AND THE WELL
∞
BRER RABBIT AND THE PEANUT PATCH
∞
BRER RABBIT AND THE RIDING HORSE
∞
BRER RABBIT'S GOOD CHILDREN
∞
HOW MISS COW WAS MILKED
∞
FISHING FOR THE MOON

Many years ago on a cotton plantation down in the deep south of North America there lived an old black slave called Uncle Remus. Every evening he would sit in his creaky old rocking chair on the shady verandah and tell his tales to anyone who would care to listen. With eyes as round as saucers, the little children gathered around his feet and when Uncle Remus was quite comfortable he would begin.

He told about the days long, long ago when animals would stroll around town arm in arm, talking and laughing just the same as us folks. Some of the animals were good little animals, and some of them were bad. And some of them were so full of mischief there was no telling just what they might do next. Just the same as us folks, you could say!

These are just a few of those stories that Uncle Remus first told all those years ago.

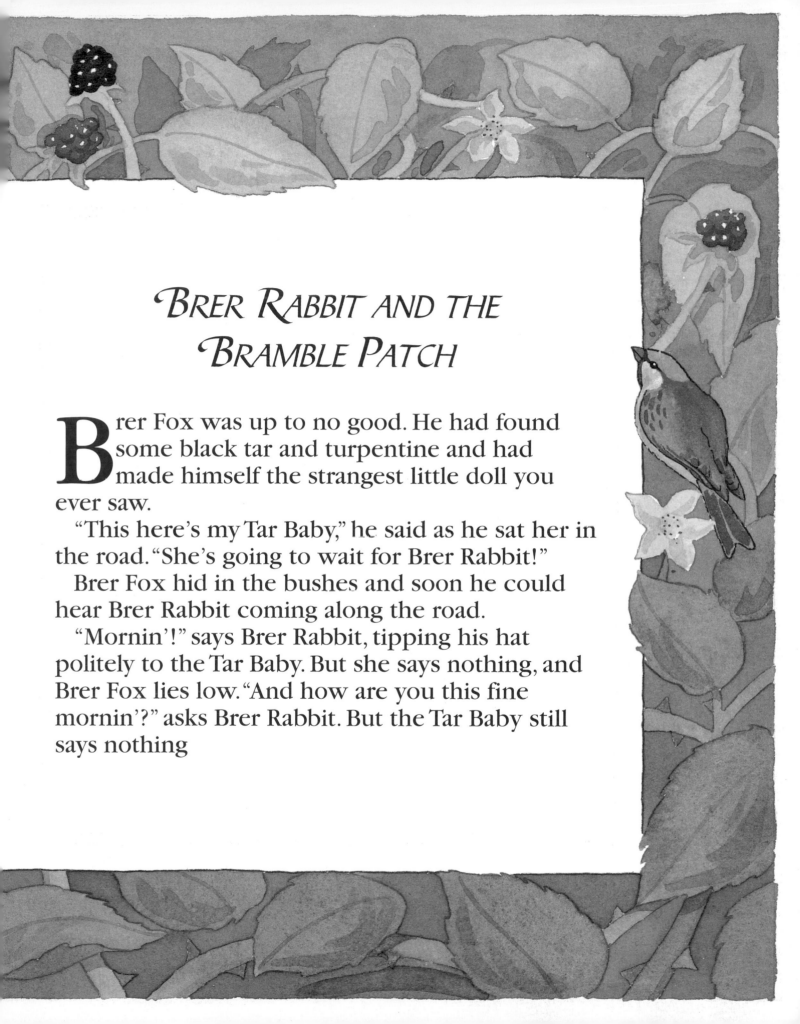

BRER RABBIT AND THE BRAMBLE PATCH

Brer Fox was up to no good. He had found some black tar and turpentine and had made himself the strangest little doll you ever saw.

"This here's my Tar Baby," he said as he sat her in the road. "She's going to wait for Brer Rabbit!"

Brer Fox hid in the bushes and soon he could hear Brer Rabbit coming along the road.

"Mornin'!" says Brer Rabbit, tipping his hat politely to the Tar Baby. But she says nothing, and Brer Fox lies low. "And how are you this fine mornin'?" asks Brer Rabbit. But the Tar Baby still says nothing

"If you don't say howdy to me I'm gonna bust your nose!" shouted Brer Rabbit, and blip! he smacked the Tar Baby on the side of her head. Well, that was a big mistake for now his hand was stuck. He smacked the Tar Baby again. Second big mistake!

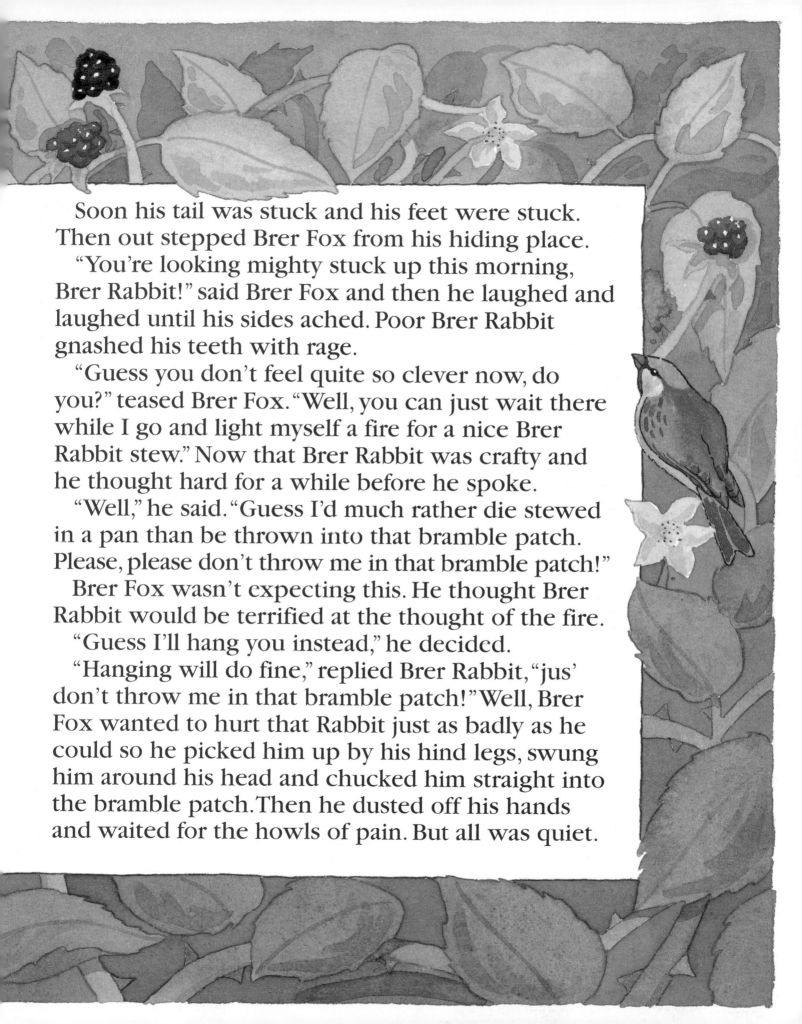

Soon his tail was stuck and his feet were stuck. Then out stepped Brer Fox from his hiding place.

"You're looking mighty stuck up this morning, Brer Rabbit!" said Brer Fox and then he laughed and laughed until his sides ached. Poor Brer Rabbit gnashed his teeth with rage.

"Guess you don't feel quite so clever now, do you?" teased Brer Fox. "Well, you can just wait there while I go and light myself a fire for a nice Brer Rabbit stew." Now that Brer Rabbit was crafty and he thought hard for a while before he spoke.

"Well," he said. "Guess I'd much rather die stewed in a pan than be thrown into that bramble patch. Please, please don't throw me in that bramble patch!"

Brer Fox wasn't expecting this. He thought Brer Rabbit would be terrified at the thought of the fire.

"Guess I'll hang you instead," he decided.

"Hanging will do fine," replied Brer Rabbit, "jus' don't throw me in that bramble patch!" Well, Brer Fox wanted to hurt that Rabbit just as badly as he could so he picked him up by his hind legs, swung him around his head and chucked him straight into the bramble patch. Then he dusted off his hands and waited for the howls of pain. But all was quiet.

After a while he heard Brer Rabbit's voice calling out to him quite cheerfully from the top of the hill.

"Why, thanks Brer Fox," he cried. "Thanks for setting me free from that Tar Baby. And thanks for dropping me off in that old bramble patch. Why, that's one of my very favourite places, you know! I was born and raised in that bramble patch!"

Brer Rabbit and the Well

Brer Rabbit was hard at work in the garden with Brer Fox, Brer Raccoon and Brer Bear. The sun was hot and he was fed up.

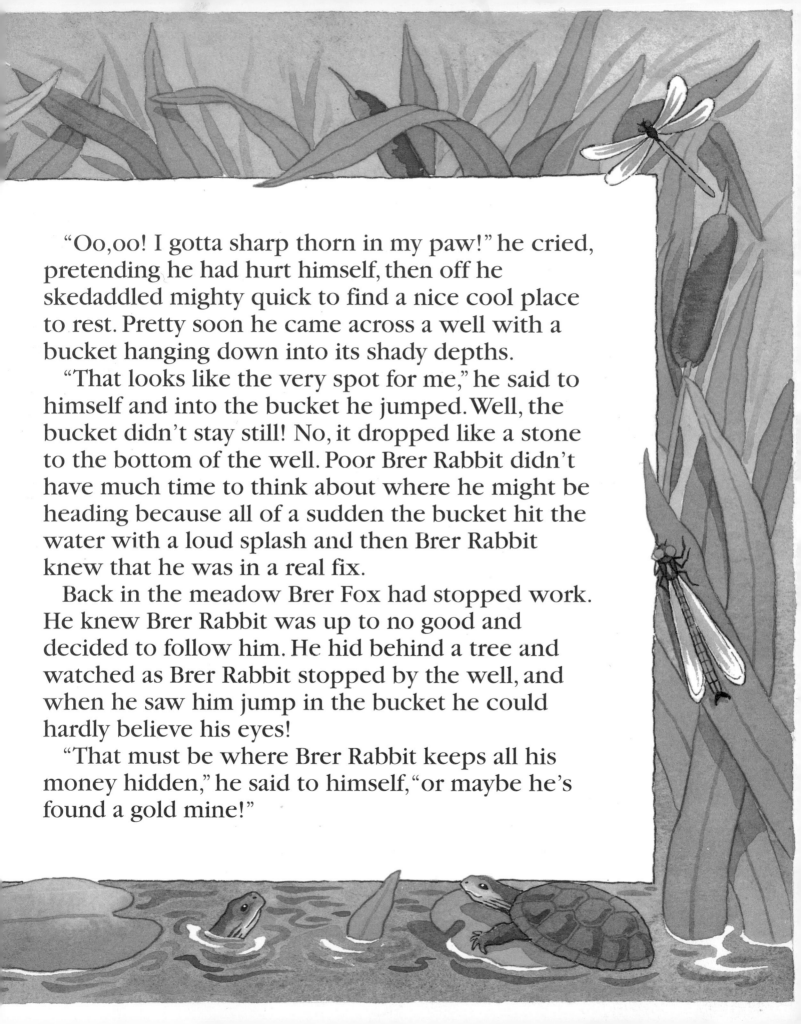

"Oo, oo! I gotta sharp thorn in my paw!" he cried, pretending he had hurt himself, then off he skedaddled mighty quick to find a nice cool place to rest. Pretty soon he came across a well with a bucket hanging down into its shady depths.

"That looks like the very spot for me," he said to himself and into the bucket he jumped. Well, the bucket didn't stay still! No, it dropped like a stone to the bottom of the well. Poor Brer Rabbit didn't have much time to think about where he might be heading because all of a sudden the bucket hit the water with a loud splash and then Brer Rabbit knew that he was in a real fix.

Back in the meadow Brer Fox had stopped work. He knew Brer Rabbit was up to no good and decided to follow him. He hid behind a tree and watched as Brer Rabbit stopped by the well, and when he saw him jump in the bucket he could hardly believe his eyes!

"That must be where Brer Rabbit keeps all his money hidden," he said to himself, "or maybe he's found a gold mine!"

Slowly he crept to the well and peered over the edge. There wasn't a sound to be heard. Down at the bottom of the well poor Brer Rabbit sat hunched up in his bucket, hardly daring to twitch a whisker. Suddenly a loud voice echoed down the well.

"Howdy, Brer Rabbit," called Brer Fox. "What are you doing down there?" Brer Rabbit thought hard.

"I'm fishing," he replied. "There are some mighty fine fish down here, Brer Fox. Why don't you come and get some for yourself?"

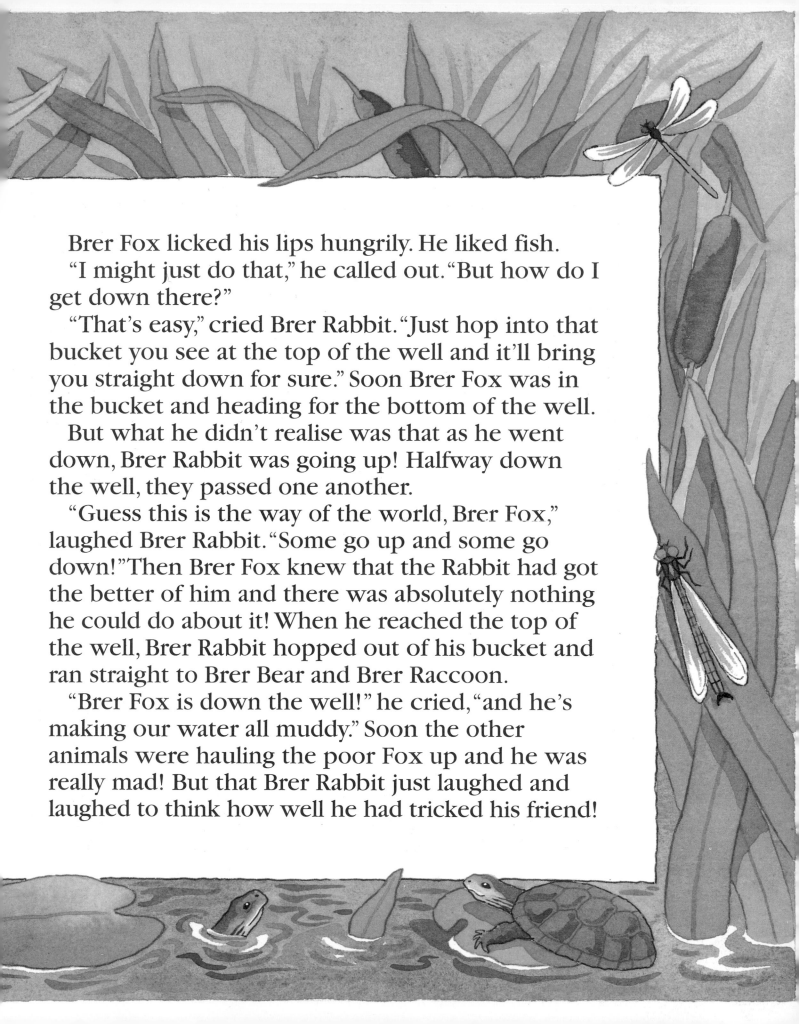

Brer Fox licked his lips hungrily. He liked fish.

"I might just do that," he called out. "But how do I get down there?"

"That's easy," cried Brer Rabbit. "Just hop into that bucket you see at the top of the well and it'll bring you straight down for sure." Soon Brer Fox was in the bucket and heading for the bottom of the well.

But what he didn't realise was that as he went down, Brer Rabbit was going up! Halfway down the well, they passed one another.

"Guess this is the way of the world, Brer Fox," laughed Brer Rabbit. "Some go up and some go down!" Then Brer Fox knew that the Rabbit had got the better of him and there was absolutely nothing he could do about it! When he reached the top of the well, Brer Rabbit hopped out of his bucket and ran straight to Brer Bear and Brer Raccoon.

"Brer Fox is down the well!" he cried, "and he's making our water all muddy." Soon the other animals were hauling the poor Fox up and he was really mad! But that Brer Rabbit just laughed and laughed to think how well he had tricked his friend!

BRER RABBIT AND THE PEANUT PATCH

Brer Fox was mighty proud of his peanut patch. He weeded it and watered it and looked forward very much to the day when he could eat a fine crop of nuts. But Brer Rabbit had his eye on that self same peanut patch and one morning, when the peanuts had grown big and ripe, he crept through the fence and helped himself just as sassy as you please.

When Brer Fox saw that somebody had been scrabbling in and out of his plants he grew mighty mad.

"I'm going to make a trap and catch that no-good varmint who's stealing my peanuts if it's the last thing I do," he said to himself. Soon he had made a fine trap with some rope and a slim hickory sapling and he positioned it right next to the hole in the fence.

The very next day Brer Rabbit came sashaying down the road towards the peanut patch. He wriggled all unsuspecting through the hole in the fence and what a fright he got when he suddenly found himself whisked up in the air and dangling by his back paws on the end of a rope! There he swung, to and fro, while he tried his best to think of a way to free himself.

Just then Brer Bear came ambling down the road. "Howdy, Brer Bear!" called Brer Rabbit.

"What in tarnation are you doin' up there?" asked the astonished Bear as he spotted Brer Rabbit above him.

"Why, I'm earning a dollar a minute guarding the peanut patch for Brer Fox," replied the wily Rabbit. "But I reckon I've earned enough money now," he added. "Do you want to take over from me?"

Brer Bear looked at him doubtfully. "Do you reckon I could do it?" he said. Brer Rabbit nodded encouragingly.

"Why, it's easy as pie," he said. "I'll show you what to do!"

Soon Brer Rabbit was standing on the ground and Brer Bear was swinging in the air.

"Brer Fox, come out!" shouted the naughty Rabbit. "Here's the rascal who's been stealing your peanuts!" Out shot Brer Fox with a stout stick in his hand.

"So that's your game, is it?" he cried, and he set about poor Brer Bear with his stick. The Bear tried in vain to explain that he was guarding his peanut patch for him but the furious Brer Fox did not believe a single word of it.

And where was Brer Rabbit? Why, he was long gone. Long gone!

BRER RABBIT AND THE
RIDING HORSE

Brer Rabbit and Brer Fox were at it again. No matter what one of them did, the other had to try and do it just a little bit better.

One day Brer Rabbit was taking tea with his good friend, Miss Meadows. "I feel sorry for that pesky Brer Fox," he confided. "When I see the poor thing struggling to keep up with me it makes me want to weep. He's just not in my league." He shook his head pityingly. "Foxes have always been inferior to Rabbits. Why, my daddy used to use Brer Fox as his riding horse many years ago."

Miss Meadows looked most astonished to hear this news and when Brer Fox next came to call she asked him if it was indeed true that he used to be Brer Rabbit's father's riding horse. Brer Fox grew red with rage and it took some time before he could talk.

"Miss Meadows," he said at last. "I am gonna make that Brer Rabbit eat those words and spit them out!"

Soon Brer Fox was hammering upon Brer Rabbit's front door. Brer Rabbit wanted him to go away so he called out of the window.

"I am glad you are here, Brer Fox!" he said. "Please run and fetch me the doctor for I am ill."

"Well, isn't that a shame," replied Brer Fox, "because Miss Meadows and the girls are having a party and they would dearly love you to come." Then Brer Rabbit thought for a while.

"I am not well enough to walk," he said. "You will have to carry me upon your back." Brer Fox didn't like this idea at all but he finally gave in.

"I will need a saddle and a bridle," added Brer Rabbit. "I shouldn't want to fall off before I get there." Soon Brer Fox was fully kitted up with saddle and bridle and Brer Rabbit sat squarely on his back looking for all the world like a regular race jockey. And then he had some fun! He dug in his heels and that poor Brer Fox had no choice but to gallop off down the road.

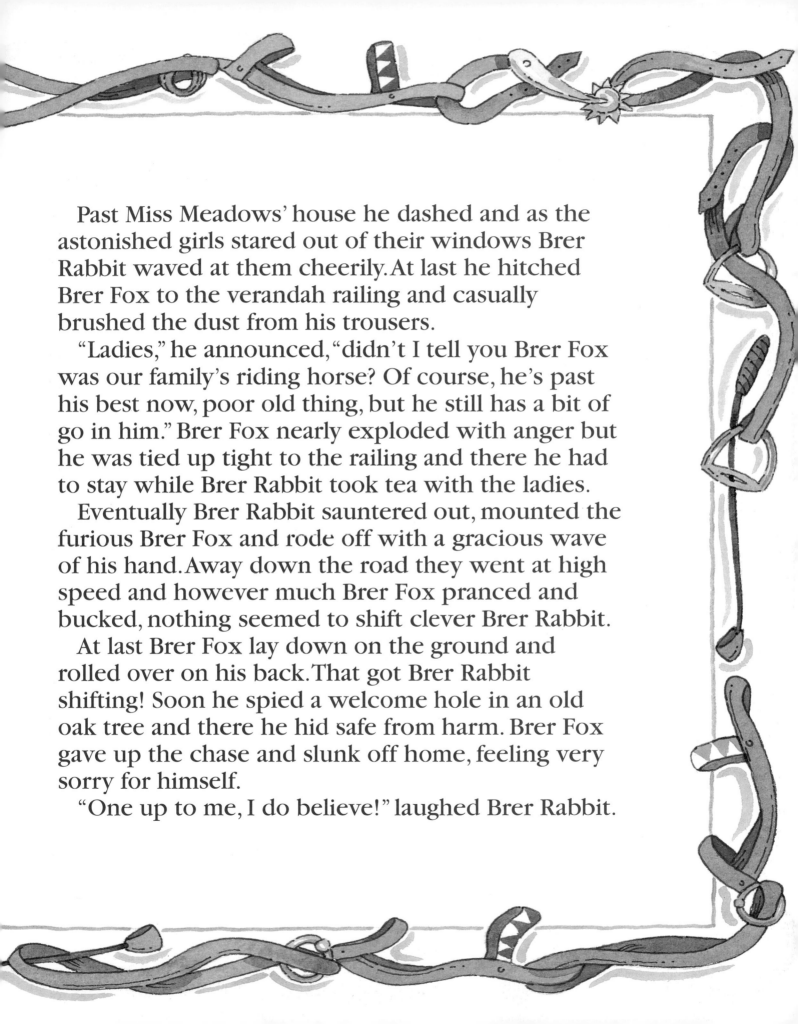

Past Miss Meadows' house he dashed and as the astonished girls stared out of their windows Brer Rabbit waved at them cheerily. At last he hitched Brer Fox to the verandah railing and casually brushed the dust from his trousers.

"Ladies," he announced, "didn't I tell you Brer Fox was our family's riding horse? Of course, he's past his best now, poor old thing, but he still has a bit of go in him." Brer Fox nearly exploded with anger but he was tied up tight to the railing and there he had to stay while Brer Rabbit took tea with the ladies.

Eventually Brer Rabbit sauntered out, mounted the furious Brer Fox and rode off with a gracious wave of his hand. Away down the road they went at high speed and however much Brer Fox pranced and bucked, nothing seemed to shift clever Brer Rabbit.

At last Brer Fox lay down on the ground and rolled over on his back. That got Brer Rabbit shifting! Soon he spied a welcome hole in an old oak tree and there he hid safe from harm. Brer Fox gave up the chase and slunk off home, feeling very sorry for himself.

"One up to me, I do believe!" laughed Brer Rabbit.

BRER RABBIT'S GOOD CHILDREN

Brer Fox was hungry. His tummy was a-rumbling and a-grumbling and he knew the only way to quieten it was to find some food.

"I wonder if Brer Rabbit has any tasty titbits hidden away inside his house?" Brer Fox wondered and he peeked inside the window. There he saw Brer Rabbit's children frisking about their hole without a care in the world. The hungry Fox licked his lips.

He knew that the little rabbits were all alone because he had just seen Brer Rabbit and Mrs Rabbit inspecting Brer Turtle's cabbage patch. He tapped on the glass with his paw.

"Let me in," called Brer Fox in a wheedling voice, "and I'll just sit and wait for your ole daddy to come home." Now these little rabbits knew Brer Fox and they were polite little rabbits, so they opened the door and pretty soon Brer Fox was sitting comfortably and watching them with a strange look in his eye.

Presently he pointed at a large piece of sugar cane leaning up against the wall.

"I sure am hungry," he said. "Break me off a piece of that cane, will you?" Now Brer Fox knew there isn't anything much tougher in the world than sugar cane and he hoped the rabbits would fail, for then he would have an excuse to eat them. The little bunnies pushed and pulled at the cane but it wouldn't even bend. Just then they heard a bird on the roof singing to them.

"Use your toofies and gnaw it and then it will break."

So the rabbits set to with their sharp teeth and soon they laid a sweet, juicy piece of cane at Brer Fox's feet.

Brer Fox thought again. He would have to find them something harder to do. Then he saw a sieve on the wall.

"I'm mighty thirsty, rabbits!" said he. "Take that sieve and fetch me some water from the spring." The rabbits ran down and dipped the sieve in the water, but to their dismay the water just trickled straight out again. Then they heard the little bird singing once again.

"Line it with clay, then the water will stay."

The rabbits did as they were told and soon they had carried a sieve full of water back to Brer Fox. He was furious to see that this plan had also failed.

Then he spied a large log lying in the woodpile.
"Right, you rabs," he said, just a touch testily. "I'm
feeling kinda chilly. Put that log on the fire and
warm me up." But no matter how hard the little
rabbits pushed at the big log, it just would not
move. Then the bird sang for a third time.

"All get behind it and push it and pole it.
Spit on your paws and rock it and roll it."

So the rabbits all worked together and soon that
log was blazing on top of the fire. Brer Fox
gnashed his teeth. He felt hungrier than ever!

Just then who should walk in but Brer Rabbit himself and my, how his little children were pleased to see him. He took just one look at Brer Fox and knew straightaway what he was up to.

"Do stay and have tea with us, Brer Fox," offered Brer Rabbit. "You look mighty peckish." But something in Brer Rabbit's voice made Brer Fox want to get out of the house as quickly as possible and with a sheepish grin he made his excuses and left.

HOW MISS COW WAS MILKED

Brer Rabbit was thirsty. He watched Miss Cow grazing peacefully in the meadow. He would love a drink of milk, but how was he to get it? "Howdy, Sis Cow," he said after a while.

"Could you do me a little favour, Sis Cow?" Brer Rabbit went on, all big eyes and innocence. Miss Cow stopped chewing and looked up at him.

"I would dearly love to eat some of those persimmons," explained Brer Rabbit, pointing to a large tree growing in the meadow. "If you shake the trunk, then they will fall down off the branches and we can share them."

Now Miss Cow was a friendly creature and all too happy to oblige. She ran at that tree full tilt, but what a shock she had when her horn got stuck in the trunk!

Off ran that wily Brer Rabbit and pretty soon he was back with all his little children and each one carried a clanking milk pail! The children clustered so tight around Miss Cow that you could hardly see her and right in the very centre of them sat Brer Rabbit on a three legged stool, milking away for all he was worth.

He filled pail after pail with the sweet warm milk and when he was done he tipped his hat politely.

"I realised you might be stuck there all night and figured that you'd be pretty sore carrying all that milk, so I thought I'd help you out. Kind of a good deed, you might say," and with that he set off for home.

Miss Cow was furious! With one mighty moo, she pawed at the ground and pulled her horn free. Why, she was so mad that Brer Rabbit could have sworn he saw real steam coming from her nostrils!

She raced down the meadow after him and the earth trembled under her hooves. But at the bottom of the field was a large bramble patch and that lucky Rabbit was soon safe inside the bushes. How he laughed.

"There isn't one animal I know who can get the better of ole Brer Rabbit!" he boasted happily.

FISHING FOR THE MOON

One day Brer Rabbit decided to play a trick on his friends, Brer Fox, Brer Wolf and Brer Bear. "I'll invite them to meet us down at the millpond tomorrow evening and we'll go fishing," he told Brer Turtle. The next night the animals set off with their nets and rods and maggots.

But when they got to the pond Brer Rabbit gasped in amazement, then shook his head.

"I reckon they'll be no fishing for us tonight," he said, "for the moon has fallen in the water."

Sure enough, there she lay quivering in the pond and the animals all tut-tutted and scratched their heads.

"Only way we'll get some fishing done tonight is if we drag her out," said Brer Rabbit at last.

"Good idea!" agreed Brer Turtle and soon Brer Fox, Brer Bear and Brer Wolf were in the pond with a net.

"You've nearly got her!" cried Brer Rabbit as he tried hard not to laugh.

"We just can't seem to catch her!" wailed Brer Fox. Deeper and deeper they went until suddenly they were out of their depth and thrashing the water so much it was a wonder they didn't empty the pond! At last they scrambled onto the bank, quite miserable.

"Better luck next time!" said Brer Rabbit grinning broadly and he winked at Brer Turtle. Why, it was almost *too* easy to trick those silly animals!

JUST-SO STORIES

Illustrated by Jo Caine

STORIES INCLUDED IN
JUST-SO STORIES

How the Leopard got his Spots
✂
How the Rhinoceros got his Skin
✂
How the Whale got his Throat
✂
How the Camel got his Hump
✂
The Elephant's Child
✂
The Cat that Walked by Himself

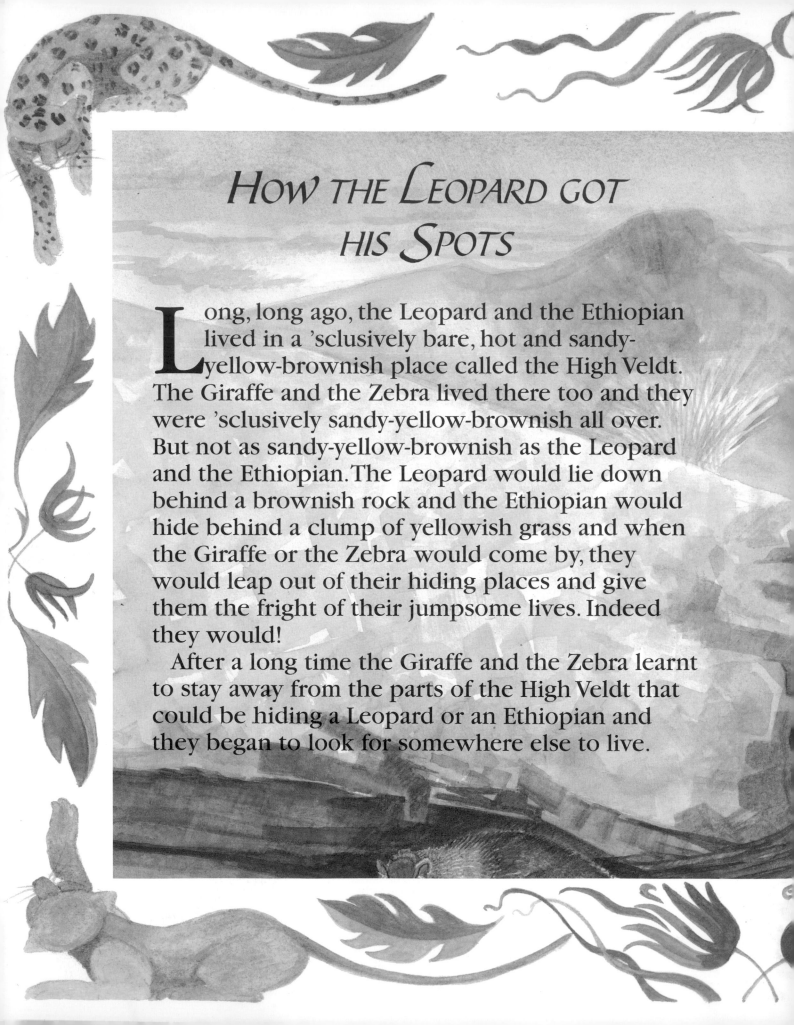

HOW THE LEOPARD GOT HIS SPOTS

Long, long ago, the Leopard and the Ethiopian lived in a 'sclusively bare, hot and sandy-yellow-brownish place called the High Veldt. The Giraffe and the Zebra lived there too and they were 'sclusively sandy-yellow-brownish all over. But not as sandy-yellow-brownish as the Leopard and the Ethiopian. The Leopard would lie down behind a brownish rock and the Ethiopian would hide behind a clump of yellowish grass and when the Giraffe or the Zebra would come by, they would leap out of their hiding places and give them the fright of their jumpsome lives. Indeed they would!

After a long time the Giraffe and the Zebra learnt to stay away from the parts of the High Veldt that could be hiding a Leopard or an Ethiopian and they began to look for somewhere else to live.

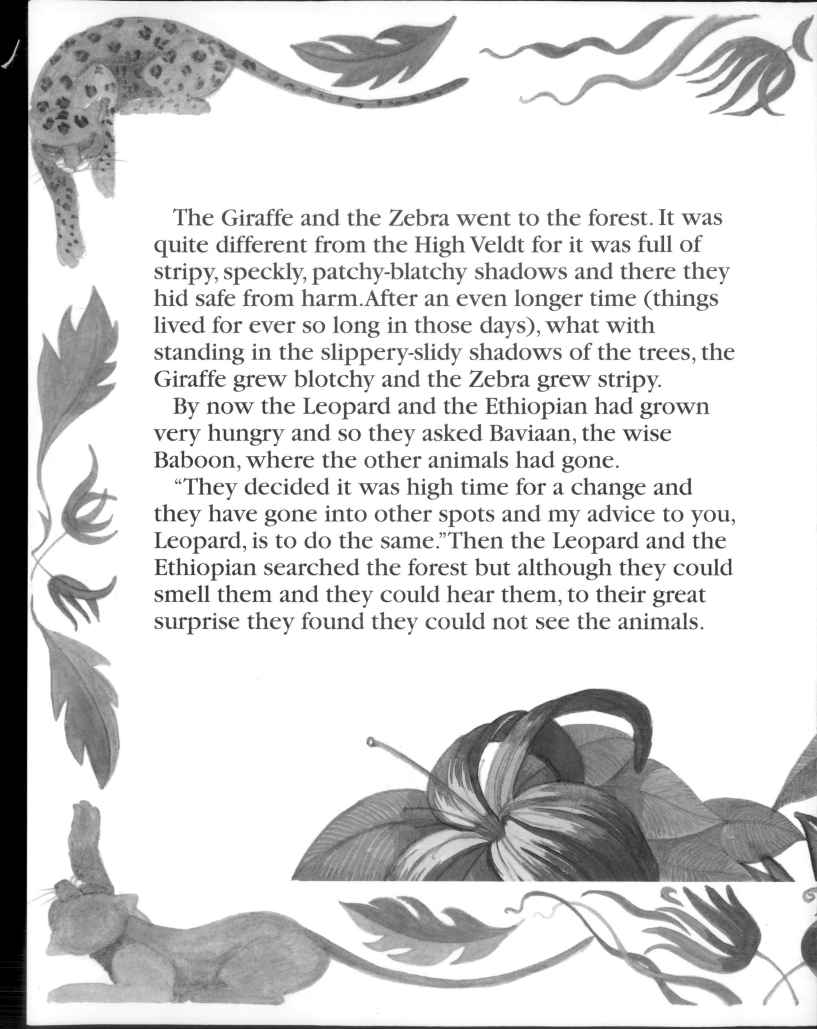

The Giraffe and the Zebra went to the forest. It was quite different from the High Veldt for it was full of stripy, speckly, patchy-blatchy shadows and there they hid safe from harm. After an even longer time (things lived for ever so long in those days), what with standing in the slippery-slidy shadows of the trees, the Giraffe grew blotchy and the Zebra grew stripy.

By now the Leopard and the Ethiopian had grown very hungry and so they asked Baviaan, the wise Baboon, where the other animals had gone.

"They decided it was high time for a change and they have gone into other spots and my advice to you, Leopard, is to do the same." Then the Leopard and the Ethiopian searched the forest but although they could smell them and they could hear them, to their great surprise they found they could not see the animals.

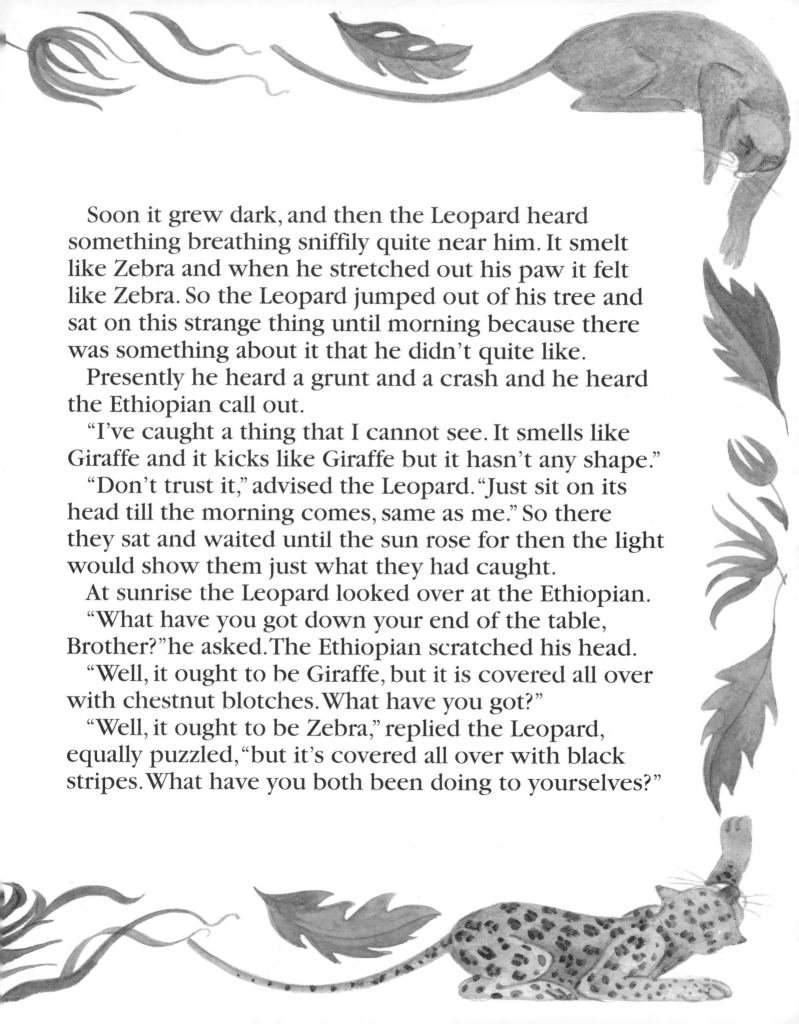

Soon it grew dark, and then the Leopard heard something breathing sniffily quite near him. It smelt like Zebra and when he stretched out his paw it felt like Zebra. So the Leopard jumped out of his tree and sat on this strange thing until morning because there was something about it that he didn't quite like.

Presently he heard a grunt and a crash and he heard the Ethiopian call out.

"I've caught a thing that I cannot see. It smells like Giraffe and it kicks like Giraffe but it hasn't any shape."

"Don't trust it," advised the Leopard. "Just sit on its head till the morning comes, same as me." So there they sat and waited until the sun rose for then the light would show them just what they had caught.

At sunrise the Leopard looked over at the Ethiopian.

"What have you got down your end of the table, Brother?" he asked. The Ethiopian scratched his head.

"Well, it ought to be Giraffe, but it is covered all over with chestnut blotches. What have you got?"

"Well, it ought to be Zebra," replied the Leopard, equally puzzled, "but it's covered all over with black stripes. What have you both been doing to yourselves?"

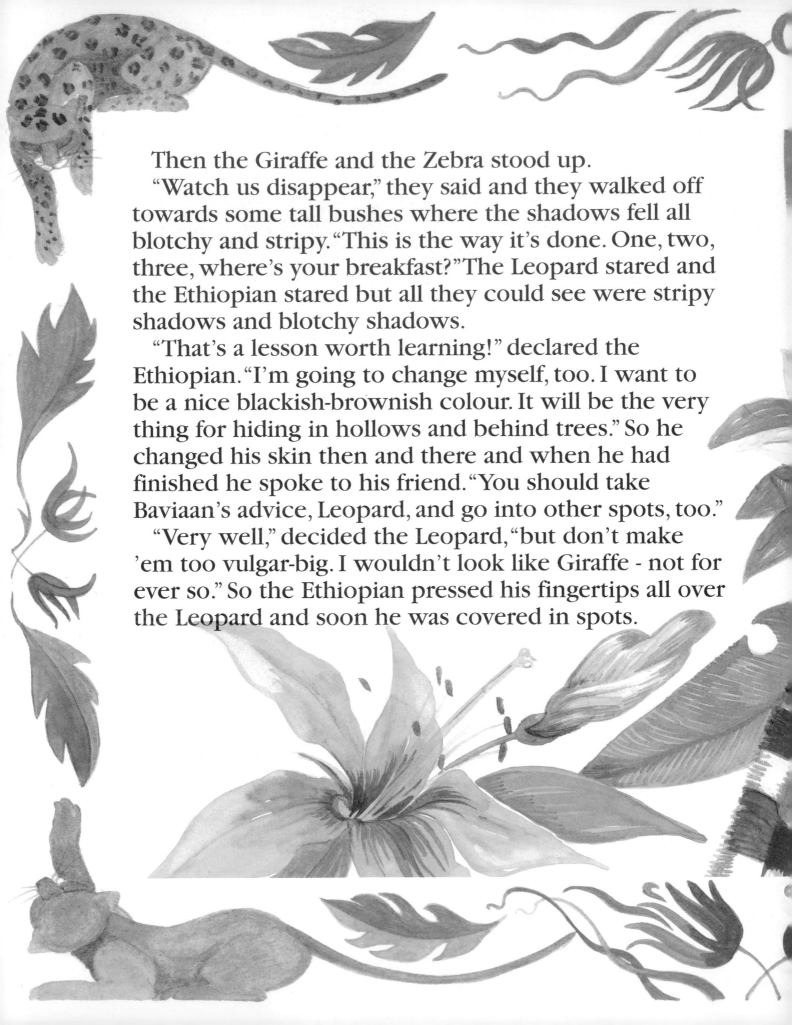

Then the Giraffe and the Zebra stood up.

"Watch us disappear," they said and they walked off towards some tall bushes where the shadows fell all blotchy and stripy. "This is the way it's done. One, two, three, where's your breakfast?" The Leopard stared and the Ethiopian stared but all they could see were stripy shadows and blotchy shadows.

"That's a lesson worth learning!" declared the Ethiopian. "I'm going to change myself, too. I want to be a nice blackish-brownish colour. It will be the very thing for hiding in hollows and behind trees." So he changed his skin then and there and when he had finished he spoke to his friend. "You should take Baviaan's advice, Leopard, and go into other spots, too."

"Very well," decided the Leopard, "but don't make 'em too vulgar-big. I wouldn't look like Giraffe - not for ever so." So the Ethiopian pressed his fingertips all over the Leopard and soon he was covered in spots.

Wherever the Ethiopian's five fingers touched his coat, they left five little black marks, all close together. Sometimes his fingers slipped and the marks got a little blurred, but if you look closely at any Leopard now you will see that there are always five spots — off five fat black fingertips.

"Now you can lie out on the ground and look like a heap of pebbles," said the Ethiopian. "You can lie on a leafy branch and look like dappled sunshine. Think of that and purr!"

And so the animals were very proud of their new coats and were very glad that they had changed. Oh, one last thing. Now and again you will hear grown-ups say, "Can the Leopard change his spots?" I don't think even grown-ups would keep on saying such a silly thing if the Leopard hadn't done it once — do you? But they will never do it again, Best Beloved. Oh no, they are quite contented just as they are.

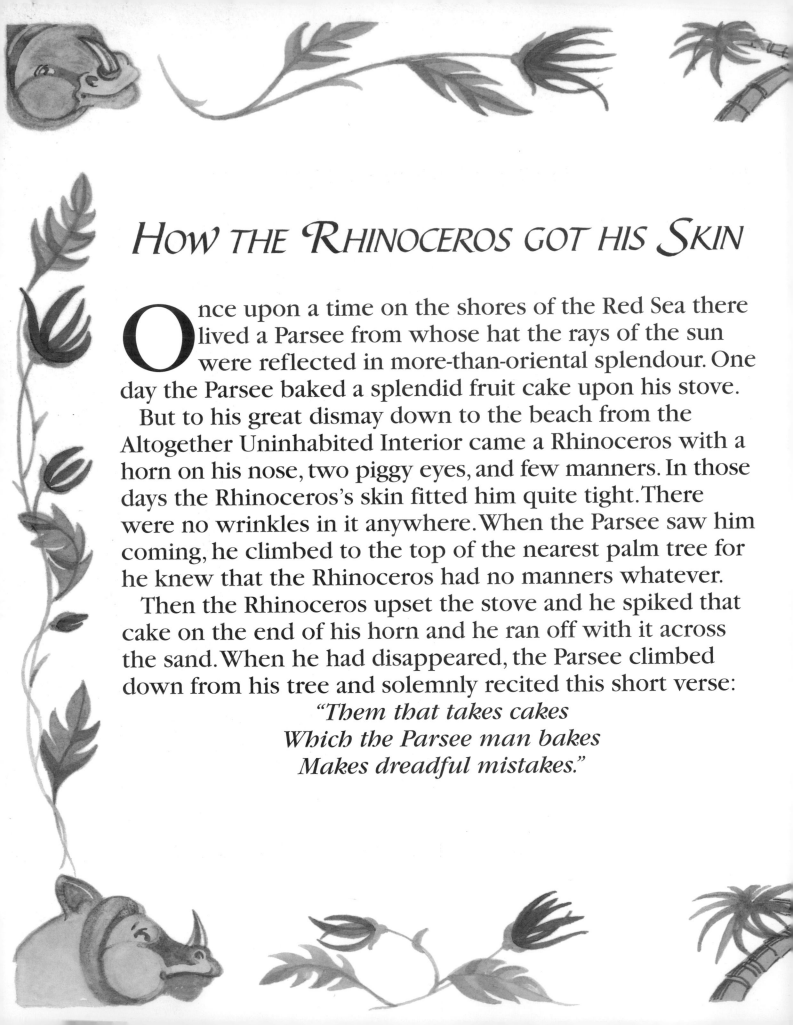

HOW THE RHINOCEROS GOT HIS SKIN

Once upon a time on the shores of the Red Sea there lived a Parsee from whose hat the rays of the sun were reflected in more-than-oriental splendour. One day the Parsee baked a splendid fruit cake upon his stove.

But to his great dismay down to the beach from the Altogether Uninhabited Interior came a Rhinoceros with a horn on his nose, two piggy eyes, and few manners. In those days the Rhinoceros's skin fitted him quite tight. There were no wrinkles in it anywhere. When the Parsee saw him coming, he climbed to the top of the nearest palm tree for he knew that the Rhinoceros had no manners whatever.

Then the Rhinoceros upset the stove and he spiked that cake on the end of his horn and he ran off with it across the sand. When he had disappeared, the Parsee climbed down from his tree and solemnly recited this short verse:

"Them that takes cakes
Which the Parsee man bakes
Makes dreadful mistakes."

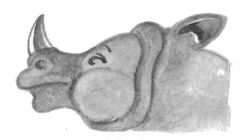

Five weeks later there was a heatwave in the Red Sea, and everybody took off all the clothes they had. The Parsee took off his hat and the Rhinoceros took off his skin and carried it over his shoulder as he went down to the beach to bathe. In those days it buttoned underneath with three buttons and looked a bit like a raincoat. He carefully laid his skin on the sand and waddled straight into the water where he had great fun blowing huge bubbles through his nose.

Presently the Parsee came by and found the skin, and he smiled a smile that ran all round his face two times. Then he went to his camp and filled his hat with cake-crumbs (for he had baked another cake). Next he took the Rhinoceros skin and he scrubbed and rubbed that skin just as full of old, dry, stale, tickly cake-crumbs as ever it could possibly hold.

Then he climbed to the top of his palm tree and waited for the Rhinoceros to come out of the water and put on his skin. And the Rhinoceros did. He buttoned it up with the three buttons, and it tickled like cake crumbs in bed. Then he wanted to scratch, but that made it worse. So he lay down on the sand and rolled and rolled and rolled, and every time he rolled, the crumbs tickled him worse and worse and worse.

Then he ran to the palm tree and rubbed and rubbed and rubbed himself against it. He rubbed so much and so hard that he rubbed his skin into a great fold over his shoulders, and another fold underneath where the buttons used to be, and he rubbed some more folds over his legs.

But it didn't make any difference to the cake crumbs. They were inside his skin and they tickled. High up at the very top of his palm tree, the Parsee hugged himself and smiled a satisfied smile.

At last the rhinoceros gave up scratching and rolling on the sand and rubbing on the tree and he went home, very angry indeed and horribly scratchy, and from that day to this every rhinoceros has great folds in his skin and a very bad temper, all on account of the cake crumbs inside.

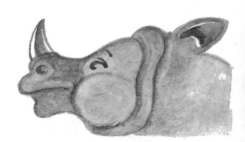

HOW THE WHALE GOT HIS THROAT

In the sea, once upon a time, was a Whale, and he ate fishes. He ate the starfish and the garfish, and the crab and the dab, and the plaice and the dace, and the skate and his mate and the mackerel and the pickereel and the really truly twirly-whirly eel. All the fishes he could find in the sea he ate with his mouth till at last there was only one small fish left, and he was a 'Stute Fish, and he swam just behind the Whale's ear so as to be out of harm's way.

"I'm hungry," complained the Whale at last. Then the 'Stute Fish said in a small 'Stute voice, "Noble and generous Cetacean, have you ever tasted Man? Man tastes nice. A bit nubbly — but nice."

"Then fetch me some," said the Whale.

"If you swim to latitude Fifty North, longitude Forty West (that is Magic), you will find, sitting on a raft, in the middle of the sea, wearing green canvas breeches and strong red braces, one shipwrecked Mariner, who, it is only fair to tell you, is a man of infinite-resource-and-sagacity," said the Fish.

Then the Whale swam to the very spot and there he swallowed the Mariner and the raft he was sitting upon and so the Mariner found himself truly inside the Whale's warm, dark inside cupboards. There he jumped and stumped and thumped and humped and he pranced and danced and banged and clanged and he hit and bit and he prowled and howled and he crawled and bawled, until the Whale felt most unhappy indeed.

"This man is very nubbly, and besides he is making me hiccough," complained the Whale to the 'Stute Fish. "I am going to get rid of him."

Then the Whale swam over the sea to the shore and he rushed halfway up the beach and opened his mouth. But while the Whale had been swimming, the Mariner had cut his raft into a square grating and he had tied it firmly inside the Whale's throat with his braces!

Then out he jumped onto the beach and spoke:

"By means of a grating I have stopped your ating."

And it was true. The Whale could no longer eat big fish or men. No, from then on all he could eat was the very smallest of tiny fish for only the smallest of fish could pass through the holes in the grating.

How the Camel got his Hump

Now this tale tells how the Camel got his big hump. In the beginning of years, when he world was so new-and-all, and the Animals were just beginning to work for Man, there lived a Camel, and he lived in the middle of a Howling Desert because he did not want to work.

He ate thorns and tamarisks and milkweed and prickles and was most 'scruciating idle, and when anybody spoke to him he said "Humph!" Just "Humph!" and no more. The Dog and the Horse and the Ox each tried to persuade him to help them with the work but the Camel would only reply "Humph!" Now the other animals thought that this was most unfair so when one day the Djinn of All Deserts came rolling along in a cloud of dust (Djinns always travel that way because it is Magic), they asked for help.

"Djinn of All Deserts," said the Horse, "is it right for any one to be idle, with the world so new-and-all? There is a thing in the middle of your Howling Desert with a long neck and long legs and he won't do a stroke of work."

Then the Djinn rolled across the desert until he found the Camel most 'scruciatingly idle, looking at his own reflection in a pool of water.

"You have given the Horse, the Dog and the Ox extra work, all on account of your 'scruciating idleness," said the Djinn sternly to the Camel.

"Humph!" the Camel replied.

"I shouldn't say that again if I was you," said the Djinn, and he began to work a Magic. Then the Camel said "Humph!" again; but no sooner had he said it than he saw his back begin to puff up and puff up into a great big lolloping humph.

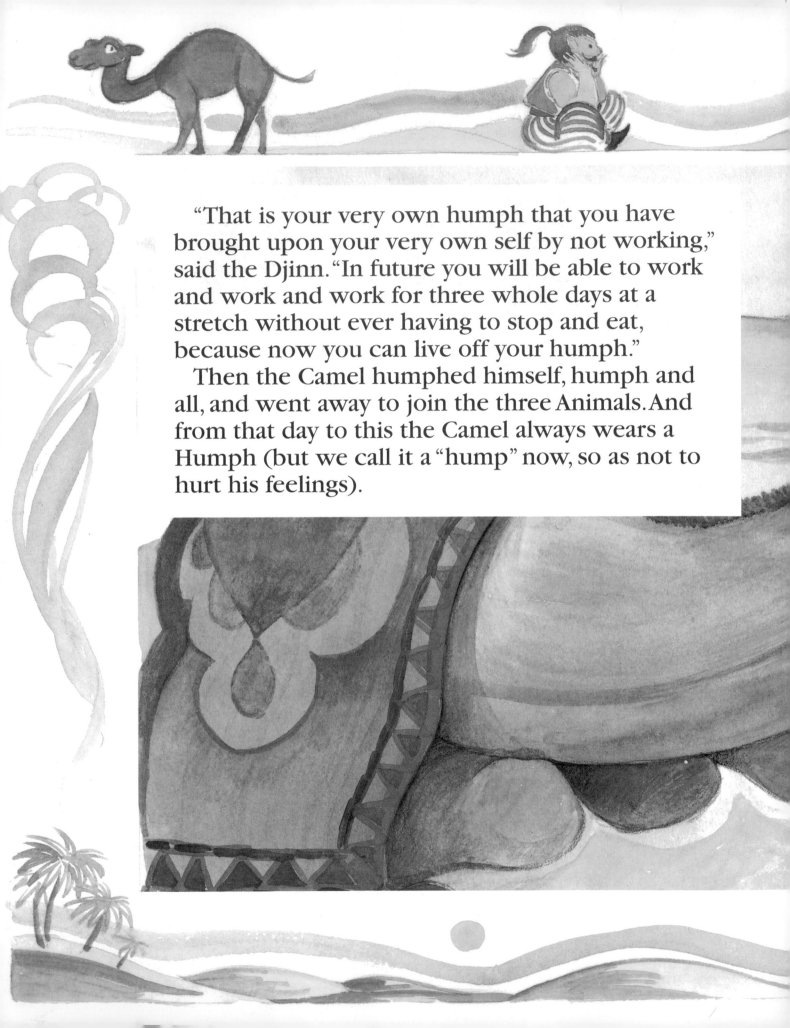

"That is your very own humph that you have brought upon your very own self by not working," said the Djinn. "In future you will be able to work and work and work for three whole days at a stretch without ever having to stop and eat, because now you can live off your humph."

Then the Camel humphed himself, humph and all, and went away to join the three Animals. And from that day to this the Camel always wears a Humph (but we call it a "hump" now, so as not to hurt his feelings).

THE ELEPHANT'S CHILD

In the High and Far-Off Times the Elephant, O Best Beloved, had no trunk. He had only a blackish, bulgy nose, as big as a boot, that he could wriggle about from side to side, but he couldn't pick up things with it. Now there was one Elephant, a new Elephant, an Elephant's Child, who was full of 'satiable curiosity — and that means he asked ever so many questions. *And* he lived in Africa and he filled all Africa with his 'satiable curtiosities.

He asked his tall aunt, the Ostrich, why her tail-feathers grew just so. He asked his tall uncle, the Giraffe, what made his skin spotty. He asked his broad aunt, the Hippopotamus, why her eyes were red and he asked his hairy uncle, the Baboon, why melons tasted just so. He asked questions about everything that he saw, or heard, or felt, or smelt, or touched, and his aunts and his uncles spanked and spanked him but *still* he was full of 'satiable curiosity!

One fine morning the Elephant's Child asked a new fine question that he had never asked before.

"What does the Crocodile have for dinner?" he said. Then everybody said "Hush!" and spanked him well.

When they had quite finished, the Elephant's Child came upon Kolokolo Bird sitting in a thorn bush.

"If you want to find out what the Crocodile has for dinner," said the Bird, "you must go to the banks of the great grey-green, greasy Limpopo River, all set about with fever-trees, and there you will find out." So the Elephant's Child set off to find the Crocodile. Now you must understand, O Best Beloved, that this 'satiable Elephant's Child had never seen a Crocodile, and did not know what one was like.

But nevertheless he set off for the Limpopo River and the first thing that he found was a Bi-Coloured-Python-Rock-Snake curled round a rock.

"'Scuse me," said the Elephant's Child most politely, "but have you seen such a thing as a Crocodile in these promiscuous parts?"

Then the Bi-Coloured-Python-Rock-Snake uncoiled himself very quickly from the rock, and spanked the Elephant's Child with his scalesome, flailsome tail, and when he had finished the Elephant's Child thanked him politely and continued on his way.

"Come hither, Little One," said the Crocodile, "for I am the Crocodile," and he wept crocodile-tears to show it was quite true. Then the Elephant's Child grew all breathless, and panted, and then he spoke.

"You are the very person I have been looking for all these long days. Will you please tell me what you have for dinner?"

"Come hither, Little One," said the Crocodile, "and I'll whisper."

Then the Elephant's Child put his head down close to the Crocodile's musky, tusky mouth, and the Crocodile caught him by his little nose, which up to that moment had been no bigger than a boot.

"I think," said the Crocodile from between his teeth, like this,"I think today I will begin with Elephant's Child!" and he pulled and he pulled and he pulled.

"Led go!" said the Elephant's Child."You are hurtig me!"Then the Bi-Coloured-Python-Rock-Snake scuffled down the bank and knotted himself in a double-clove-hitch around the Elephant's Child's legs.

And he pulled, and the Elephant's Child pulled, and the Crocodile pulled — but the Elephant's Child and the Bi-Coloured-Python-Rock-Snake pulled hardest (and by this time the poor nose was nearly five feet long!)

At last the Crocodile let go of the Elephant's Child's nose with a plop that you could hear all up and down the Limpopo. Then the Elephant's child dangled his poor pulled nose in the water.

"I am waiting for it to shrink," he explained.

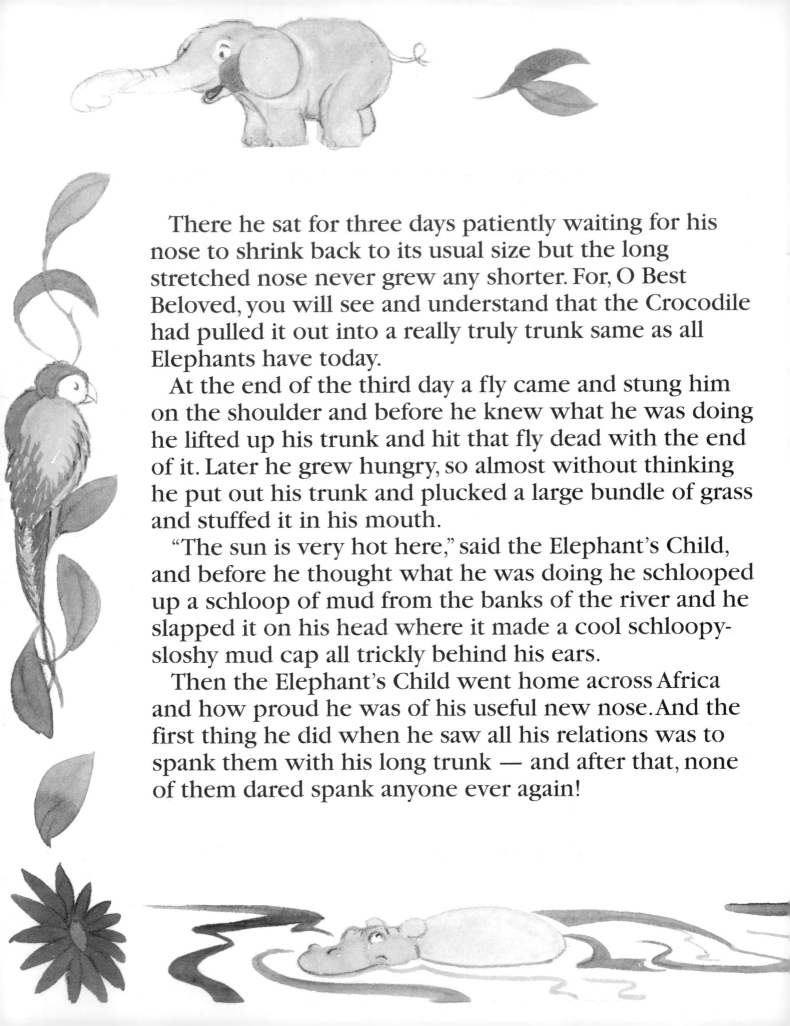

There he sat for three days patiently waiting for his nose to shrink back to its usual size but the long stretched nose never grew any shorter. For, O Best Beloved, you will see and understand that the Crocodile had pulled it out into a really truly trunk same as all Elephants have today.

At the end of the third day a fly came and stung him on the shoulder and before he knew what he was doing he lifted up his trunk and hit that fly dead with the end of it. Later he grew hungry, so almost without thinking he put out his trunk and plucked a large bundle of grass and stuffed it in his mouth.

"The sun is very hot here," said the Elephant's Child, and before he thought what he was doing he schlooped up a schloop of mud from the banks of the river and he slapped it on his head where it made a cool schloopy-sloshy mud cap all trickly behind his ears.

Then the Elephant's Child went home across Africa and how proud he was of his useful new nose. And the first thing he did when he saw all his relations was to spank them with his long trunk — and after that, none of them dared spank anyone ever again!

THE CAT THAT WALKED BY HIMSELF

Hear and attend; for this befell and behappened, O Best Beloved, when the Tame animals were wild. The Dog was wild, and the Horse was wild, and the Cow was wild, and the Sheep was wild, and the Pig was wild — as wild as wild could be — and they all walked in the Wet Wild Woods by their wild lones.

But the wildest of all the wild animals was the Cat. He walked by himself and all places were alike to him.

Of course the Man was wild too. He was dreadfully wild. He didn't even begin to be tame till he met the Woman, and she told him that she did not like living in his wild ways.

So she found a nice dry cave to lie down in and she lit a nice fire of wood at the back of the cave. Then she hung a dried wild-horse skin across the opening of the cave, and she said, "Wipe your feet, dear, when you come in, and now we'll keep house."

That night as the Man slept by the fire, the Woman sat up combing her hair. She took the bone of a shoulder of mutton and she looked at the wonderful marks that were carved on it and she made the First Singing Magic in the world. Out in the Wet Wild Woods the wild animals could see the bright light of the fire and they wondered what it meant.

Wild Dog lifted up his head and said, "I will go up and see and look. Cat, come with me."

"Nenni!" said the Cat. "I am the Cat who walks by himself, and all places are alike to me. I will not come." But after Wild Dog had set off, the Cat secretly followed him and hid himself where he could see everything.

Wild Dog entered the cave and sniffed the beautiful smell of the roast mutton and the Woman laughed.

"Here comes the first. Wild Thing out of the Wild Woods, what do you want?"

Wild Dog said, "O my Enemy and Wife of my Enemy, what is this that smells so good in the Wild Woods?" Then the Woman gave him the bone to gnaw and it was so delicious that he wanted another.

"Wild Thing out of the Wild Woods," said the Woman. "Help my Man to hunt through the day and guard this cave at night, and I will give you as many bones as you need." And so the Wild Dog became the First Friend.

"Ah!" said the Cat, listening. "This is a very wise Woman, but she is not so wise as I am."

The next night the Woman made a Second Magic and this time the Wild Horse went to see the strange light.

The Cat followed very softly and watched him enter the cave. The Woman laughed and said, "Here comes the second. Wild Thing out of the Wild Woods, what do you want?" Then the Wild Horse looked at the sweet grass that lay in a mound on the floor of the cave.

"Bend your head and wear this halter," said the Woman, "and you shall eat the grass three times a day."

"Ah!" said the Cat. "This is a clever Woman, but she is not so clever as I am."

When the Man and the Dog came back from hunting, the Man said, "What is Wild Horse doing here?"

And the Woman said, "He is now the First Servant and he will carry us from place to place for always."

The next day the Woman made her Third Magic and this time the Wild Cow came up to the cave and she promised to give her milk to the Woman every day in return for the wonderful grass. The Cat went back through the Wet Wild Woods and he never told anybody what he had seen.

But in the morning he went back to the cave and he saw the light of the fire and he smelt the warm milk. Then the Woman laughed and said, "Wild Thing out of the Wild Woods, go away for I have put away the magic bone, and we have no more need of either friends or servants in our cave."

Cat said, "I am not a friend, and I am not a servant. I am the Cat who walks by himself, and I wish to come in."

"No," said the Woman. "If you are the Cat who walks by himself, all places are alike to you. Go away and walk by yourself in all places alike." But the Cat liked the warm cave and he spoke again.

"You are very wise and beautiful," he said. "You should not be cruel, even to a Cat." Then the Woman laughed.

"I knew I was wise, but I did not know I was beautiful. So I will make a bargain with you. If ever I say one word in your praise, you may come into the cave. And if ever I say two words in your praise, you may sit by the fire. And if ever I say three words in your praise, you may drink the warm milk for always and always."

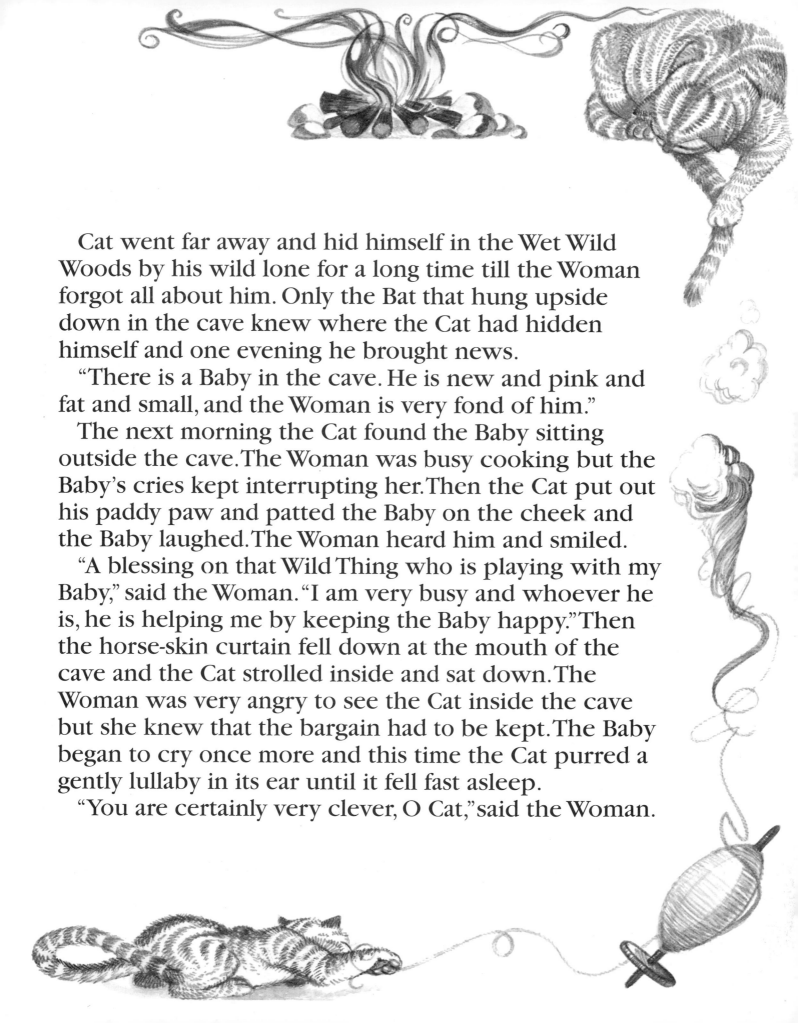

Cat went far away and hid himself in the Wet Wild Woods by his wild lone for a long time till the Woman forgot all about him. Only the Bat that hung upside down in the cave knew where the Cat had hidden himself and one evening he brought news.

"There is a Baby in the cave. He is new and pink and fat and small, and the Woman is very fond of him."

The next morning the Cat found the Baby sitting outside the cave. The Woman was busy cooking but the Baby's cries kept interrupting her. Then the Cat put out his paddy paw and patted the Baby on the cheek and the Baby laughed. The Woman heard him and smiled.

"A blessing on that Wild Thing who is playing with my Baby," said the Woman. "I am very busy and whoever he is, he is helping me by keeping the Baby happy." Then the horse-skin curtain fell down at the mouth of the cave and the Cat strolled inside and sat down. The Woman was very angry to see the Cat inside the cave but she knew that the bargain had to be kept. The Baby began to cry once more and this time the Cat purred a gently lullaby in its ear until it fell fast asleep.

"You are certainly very clever, O Cat," said the Woman.

Then the smoke suddenly puffed up from the fire and when it had cleared, there sat the Cat sitting quite comfy close to the heat of the flames.

"Now I can sit by the warm fire for always and always," said the Cat, "but still I am the Cat who walks by himself, and all places are alike to me." But the Woman was very angry and promised herself she would not say a third word in praise of the Cat.

By and by the cave grew so still that a little mouse crept out of a corner and ran across the floor.

"Ouh! Chee!" cried the Woman, and she jumped upon a stool. Then the Cat made one pounce and caught the little mouse in his claws.

"A hundred thanks," said the Woman. "You must be very wise to catch a mouse so easily."

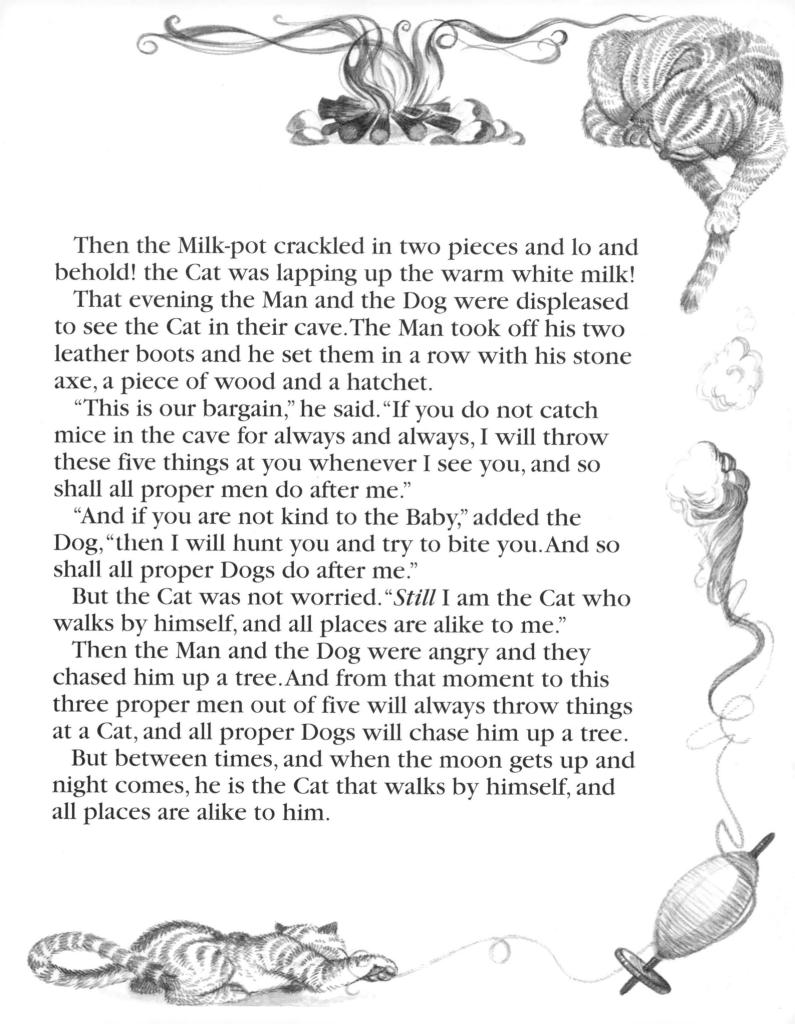

Then the Milk-pot crackled in two pieces and lo and behold! the Cat was lapping up the warm white milk!

That evening the Man and the Dog were displeased to see the Cat in their cave. The Man took off his two leather boots and he set them in a row with his stone axe, a piece of wood and a hatchet.

"This is our bargain," he said. "If you do not catch mice in the cave for always and always, I will throw these five things at you whenever I see you, and so shall all proper men do after me."

"And if you are not kind to the Baby," added the Dog, "then I will hunt you and try to bite you. And so shall all proper Dogs do after me."

But the Cat was not worried. "*Still* I am the Cat who walks by himself, and all places are alike to me."

Then the Man and the Dog were angry and they chased him up a tree. And from that moment to this three proper men out of five will always throw things at a Cat, and all proper Dogs will chase him up a tree.

But between times, and when the moon gets up and night comes, he is the Cat that walks by himself, and all places are alike to him.

NURSERY TALES

Illustrated by David Anstey, Nigel McMullen Jenny Press and Martin Aitchinson

STORIES INCLUDED IN
NURSERY TALES:

JACK AND THE BEANSTALK
∽
GOLDILOCKS AND THE THREE BEARS
∽
THE THREE LITTLE PIGS
∽
LITTLE RED RIDING HOOD
∽
THE THREE BILLY GOATS GRUFF

JACK AND THE BEANSTALK
Illustrated by David Anstey

Once upon a time there lived a poor widow woman and her son Jack. He was a lazy boy and he would not tend the crops in the field. Soon the plants died and then they had no food to eat.

"All we have left to sell is our cow," said Jack's mother, and so the next day Jack set off down the road to the market. After a while he met a pedlar.

"I will buy your cow," offered the pedlar, "and in return I will give you these special beans," and he held out his hand. Jack inspected the six speckled beans.

"It's a deal," said Jack and he hurried back home again.

But when he showed his mother what he had been paid for the cow she was very angry! She boxed his ears and threw the beans straight out of the window.

"We cannot live on a handful of beans!" she cried, and they went to bed that night very hungry indeed. But when Jack awoke the next morning the first thing he saw when he opened his eyes were huge green leaves dangling outside his bedroom window.

"Look, mother!" he shouted. "The beans have taken root and grown into an enormous plant." Indeed the beanstalk was so tall that it towered high into the sky.

"I am going to climb up and see where the stalk ends," decided Jack. Soon he was as high as the roof.

"Come back! Come back!" called his mother, but Jack kept on climbing higher and higher and after a while the house was just a tiny spot far below him. Up and up Jack went and just when he felt his arms would drop he found himself stepping off the very last branch and onto firm ground. Nearby there stood a fine castle.

"Maybe I can get some food," thought the hungry boy. But when he knocked on the door he did not get a friendly welcome from the large lady who lived there.

"Go away!" she cried. "My husband is a fierce giant and he is particularly partial to small boys such as you." But Jack was so hungry that he begged to be allowed in, and at last the woman relented. Soon Jack found himself sitting at a huge kitchen table, happily nibbling a large piece of cheese. Suddenly the table shook and a loud roar filled the air.

"Fee, fi, fo, fum, I smell the blood of an Englishman!
Be he alive or be dead,
I'll grind his bones to make my bread!"

"Quick, quick!" whispered the terrified woman. "You must hide for my husband is coming!" Hurriedly she bundled him into the oven and there Jack sat trembling like a leaf as the enormous giant strode into the kitchen and sniffed suspiciously.

"Hush, my dear. Don't fret! It is only the smell of your breakfast!" said his wife anxiously. "Come, sit and eat your food." Jack kept as quiet as a mouse as the giant shovelled the fried egg and bacon into his mouth.

"Now bring me my hen!" shouted the ogre.

The woman quickly fetched a small brown hen and placed it upon the table in front of him.

"Lay!" ordered the giant and to Jack's great astonishment the hen clucked loudly and instantly laid an egg. But this was no ordinary egg. No, this was a *golden* egg! The giant stroked the brown hen and smiled greedily. Then he yawned loudly, laid his great head upon his arms, and was soon fast asleep.

Jack was out of the oven and across the floor in a moment. Pausing only to grab the hen, he raced from the kitchen and out of the huge castle door. He ran for the beanstalk as fast as his legs could carry him and in no time at all he was back home with the hen still tucked tightly beneath his arm.

"Look, mother!" he cried. "This hen will lay as many golden eggs as we wish. We need never go hungry again."

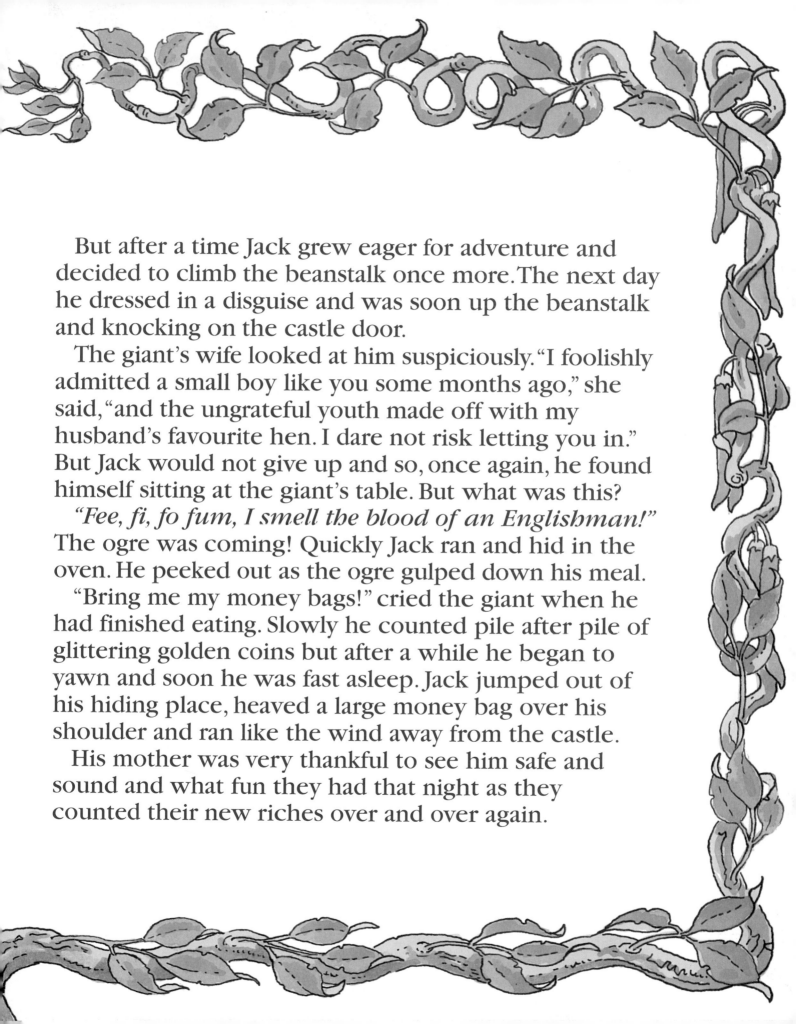

But after a time Jack grew eager for adventure and decided to climb the beanstalk once more. The next day he dressed in a disguise and was soon up the beanstalk and knocking on the castle door.

The giant's wife looked at him suspiciously. "I foolishly admitted a small boy like you some months ago," she said, "and the ungrateful youth made off with my husband's favourite hen. I dare not risk letting you in." But Jack would not give up and so, once again, he found himself sitting at the giant's table. But what was this?

"Fee, fi, fo fum, I smell the blood of an Englishman!" The ogre was coming! Quickly Jack ran and hid in the oven. He peeked out as the ogre gulped down his meal.

"Bring me my money bags!" cried the giant when he had finished eating. Slowly he counted pile after pile of glittering golden coins but after a while he began to yawn and soon he was fast asleep. Jack jumped out of his hiding place, heaved a large money bag over his shoulder and ran like the wind away from the castle.

His mother was very thankful to see him safe and sound and what fun they had that night as they counted their new riches over and over again.

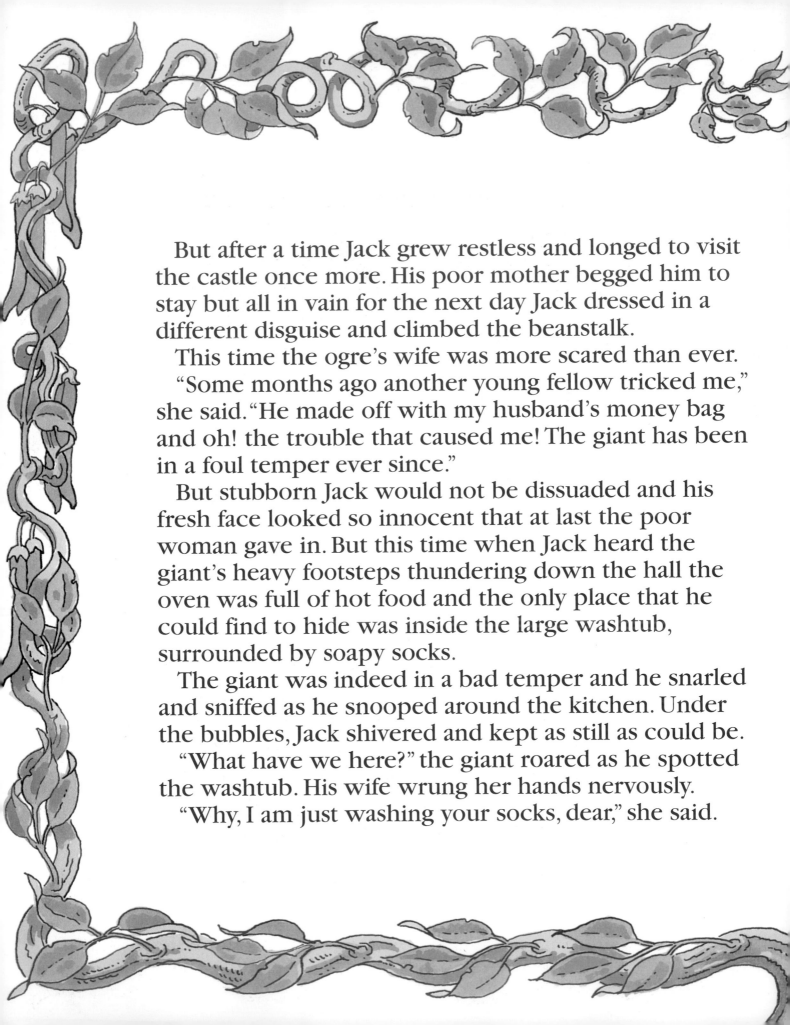

But after a time Jack grew restless and longed to visit the castle once more. His poor mother begged him to stay but all in vain for the next day Jack dressed in a different disguise and climbed the beanstalk.

This time the ogre's wife was more scared than ever.

"Some months ago another young fellow tricked me," she said. "He made off with my husband's money bag and oh! the trouble that caused me! The giant has been in a foul temper ever since."

But stubborn Jack would not be dissuaded and his fresh face looked so innocent that at last the poor woman gave in. But this time when Jack heard the giant's heavy footsteps thundering down the hall the oven was full of hot food and the only place that he could find to hide was inside the large washtub, surrounded by soapy socks.

The giant was indeed in a bad temper and he snarled and sniffed as he snooped around the kitchen. Under the bubbles, Jack shivered and kept as still as could be.

"What have we here?" the giant roared as he spotted the washtub. His wife wrung her hands nervously.

"Why, I am just washing your socks, dear," she said.

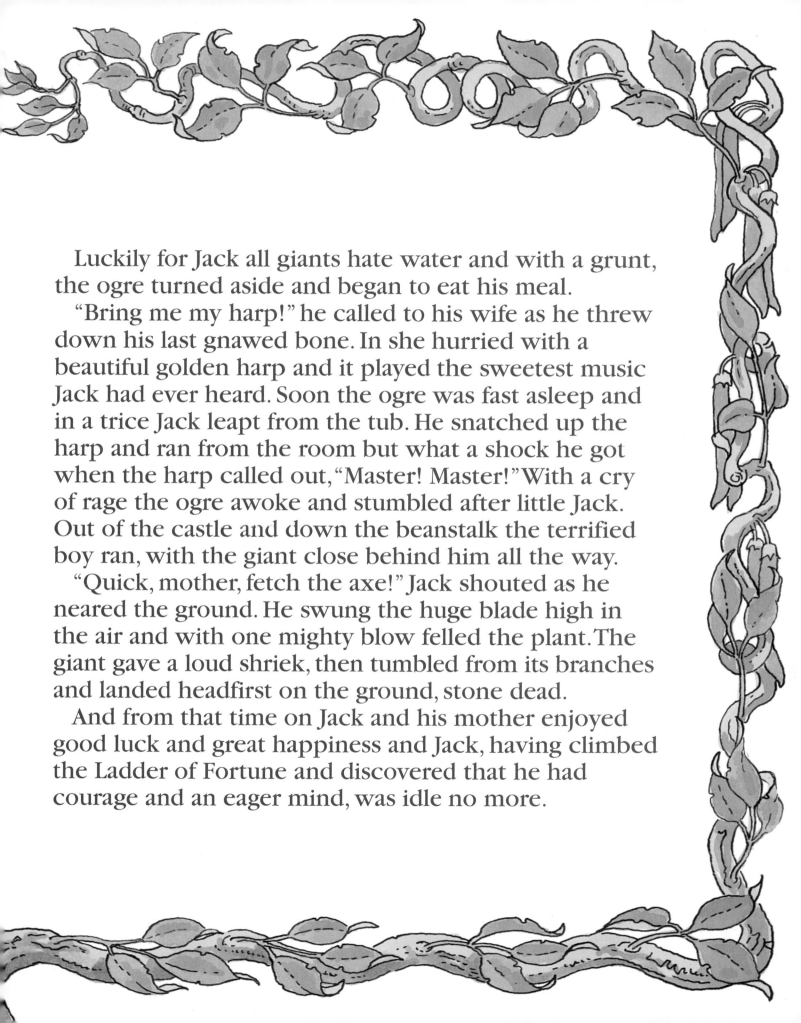

Luckily for Jack all giants hate water and with a grunt, the ogre turned aside and began to eat his meal.

"Bring me my harp!" he called to his wife as he threw down his last gnawed bone. In she hurried with a beautiful golden harp and it played the sweetest music Jack had ever heard. Soon the ogre was fast asleep and in a trice Jack leapt from the tub. He snatched up the harp and ran from the room but what a shock he got when the harp called out, "Master! Master!" With a cry of rage the ogre awoke and stumbled after little Jack. Out of the castle and down the beanstalk the terrified boy ran, with the giant close behind him all the way.

"Quick, mother, fetch the axe!" Jack shouted as he neared the ground. He swung the huge blade high in the air and with one mighty blow felled the plant. The giant gave a loud shriek, then tumbled from its branches and landed headfirst on the ground, stone dead.

And from that time on Jack and his mother enjoyed good luck and great happiness and Jack, having climbed the Ladder of Fortune and discovered that he had courage and an eager mind, was idle no more.

GOLDILOCKS AND THE THREE BEARS
Illustrated by Nigel McMullen

Once upon a time there were Three Bears. There was a large, gruff Father Bear, a middle-sized Mother Bear and a small, wee Baby Bear and they lived in a cottage in the middle of a wood.

One morning their breakfast porridge was too hot to eat so the Three Bears decided to go for a walk in the wood while it cooled down, but when they were out who should come by but little Goldilocks. She peeked in the window and saw the porridge on the table.

"Yummy!" she said. "I like porridge," and lifting the latch, she opened the door and walked inside.

First she tasted Father Bear's porridge, but that was too hot. Next she tasted Mother Bear's porridge, but that was too cold. So then she picked up Baby Bear's tiny spoon and tasted his porridge. It wasn't too hot and it wasn't too cold. It was just right!

In next to no time Baby Bear's bowl was empty. Greedy Goldilocks had eaten the porridge all up!

Now she felt so full that she decided she simply must rest a while. First she tried Father Bear's chair. It had a flat wooden seat and a high back made of thin wooden spindles. Goldilocks sat down — but she soon scrambled off again.

"What a horrid, hard chair!" she complained.

Then she tried Mother Bear's chair. It was large and squishy and filled with fat feather cushions.

"Goodness!" exclaimed Goldilocks. "Much too soft!"

Then she tried Baby Bear's little rocking chair. Father Bear had carved garden flowers into the oak wood and hidden amongst them were all the birds of the forest. Goldilocks sat down. It wasn't too hard and it wasn't too soft. It was just right!

"Perfect!" sighed Goldilocks happily, and with a tummy full of porridge and a big smile on her face, she leant back and made herself comfortable. But she was too big and too heavy for Baby Bear's little chair and with a creak and a crash it broke into tiny pieces. Goldilocks was cross!

"Maybe I can rest upstairs," she thought and up the rickety wooden stairs she went.

The bedroom was tucked right under the rafters of the roof and it was very cosy and warm. First of all Goldilocks tried Father Bear's bed but it was so high that she could not climb up into it. Then she tried Mother Bear's bed but that was so low down that Goldilocks felt as if she was lying on the floor.

"Where can I sleep?" she said to herself with a big sleepy yawn. Then she caught sight of Baby Bear's bed. It wasn't too high and it wasn't too low. It was just right! In she climbed and soon she was fast asleep.

After a while the Three Bears arrived back from their walk. They sat down at the table with rumbling tummies for they were very hungry, but they soon saw that something was wrong.

"Someone's been eating my porridge!" roared Father Bear and he looked very cross indeed.

"Someone's been eating *my* porridge!" growled Mother Bear. Then little Baby Bear looked at his plate.

"Someone's been eating *my* porridge," he squeaked, "and they've eaten it all up!"

They noticed that their chairs had been moved.

"Someone's been sitting in my chair!" said Father Bear.

"Someone's been sitting in *my* chair!" bellowed Mother Bear. Then little Baby Bear looked at his chair.

"Someone's bcen sitting in *my* chair!" he wailed, "and they've broken it into tiny pieces!"

"Whoever has done it must be hiding upstairs!" whispered Father Bear, and up the rickety wooden stairs they tiptoed, one behind the other.

"Someone's been sleeping in my bed!" grumbled Father Bear.

"Someone's been sleeping in *my* bed!" rumbled Mother Bear. Then little Baby Bear looked at his bed.

"Someone's been sleeping in *my* bed!" he squealed, "*and she's still there!*"

Then Goldilocks woke up with a start and when she saw the Three Bears looking so cross she jumped out of bed and ran like the wind down the rickety wooden stairs. Out of the door she flew and she didn't stop running until she was far away from the little cottage and the Three Bears — and after that they never saw Goldilocks again!

THE THREE LITTLE PIGS
Illustrated by Jenny Press

Once upon a time there were three little pigs. They lived at home with their mother but as the years passed they grew bigger and bigger and soon it was time for them to find homes of their own. Their mother kissed them and waved goodbye. "Watch out for the big, bad wolf!" she cried.

Soon they met a man carrying a bundle of straw.
"Please may I have some straw to build a house?"
said the first little pig, and before long he was hard
at work. The other two little pigs carried on down
the road and after a while they met a man carrying a
large bundle of sticks.
"Please may I have some sticks to build a house?"
asked the second little pig, and soon he too was hard
at work building a home for himself.

The third little pig carried on down the road and after a while he met a man carrying a load of bricks.

"Please may I have some bricks to build a house?" asked the third little pig, and soon he was very busy mixing cement and laying down brick after brick.

The first little pig finished his house of straw and shut the door. The second little pig finished his house of sticks and shut the door. The third little pig finished his house of bricks and shut the door.

"My house is good and strong," said each little pig to himself. "The wolf won't catch me now!"

The very next day who should come calling but the big, bad wolf! Down the road he prowled, peering under hedgerows and pouncing behind bushes. He was very hungry and he wanted something to eat.

When he saw the little straw house, he was most surprised.

"I wonder who lives here?" he said to himself and he peeked inside the window. How happy he was to see the first little pig sitting on the table and tucking into a large plate of porridge.

"Little pig, little pig!" he called. "Let me come in!"

The first little pig dropped his spoon in fright.
"No, no! By the hair of my chinny, chin, chin I
will *not* let you in!" he shouted.

"Then I'll huff and I'll puff and I'll blow your
house down!" roared the wolf. And he huffed
and he puffed and he *did* blow the house down
and in a trice he had eaten the first little pig all
up. Then he set off down the road. Soon he saw
the house of sticks and how delighted he was
when he spotted the second little pig sipping at
a nice cup of tea.

"Little pig, little pig, let me come in!" he cried.

"No, no! By the hair of my chinny, chin, chin I will *not* let you in!" shouted the second little pig.

"Then I'll huff and I'll puff and I'll blow your house down!" shouted the wolf and sure enough, the house blew down in no time at all and soon he had eaten the second little pig.

But when he visited the home of the third little pig he had a much harder job on his hands, for this house was made of bricks and however hard he huffed and puffed he could not blow it down. The wily wolf sat on the gate and tried to think of another plan to catch the clever little pig.

After a while the wolf knocked on his door.

"Oh, little pig," he called softly. "I know you like turnips and if you can be ready tomorrow morning at six o'clock then I will take you to Farmer Smith's field and help you pull some up." Well, the little pig was not going to fall for a trap like that and so he got up the next day and went to the field at *five* o'clock and was home cooking his turnips by the time the wolf knocked upon his door.

"You're too late," he called out. "I'm already cooking my dinner." Then the wolf gnashed his teeth and tried hard to think of another plan.

"Oh, little pig," he called. "I know you like apples so meet me at Merrygarden Farm at five o'clock in the morning and I will help you pick some." The next day the little pig went to the farm at *four* o'clock but the wolf, too, arrived early and caught him up a tree!

"Here, catch!" cried the clever pig, and he threw an apple across the meadow. The silly wolf went bounding after it and in a trice the pig was running for home. The wolf hid his anger and tried again.

"Meet me at the fair at three o'clock" he said.

But the pig went at *two* o'clock and bought a lovely butter churn. He was on his way home again when he saw the wolf coming up the hill towards him. There was nowhere to hide and so he jumped inside his barrel and rolled down the road. He thundered past the wolf and the noise frightened the poor beast so much that he turned tail and fled.

That evening the wolf knocked on the pig's door.

"A horrible monster attacked me today," he said in a quaky voice, and then the pig laughed and laughed.

"That was me in my butter churn!" he said. The wolf was furious and he climbed up on top of the roof.

"I am coming down your chimney to get you!" he cried. Quickly the pig put a large pot of water on his fire and as the wolf scrabbled down the chimney it boiled up good and hot. Splash! The wolf fell in the scalding water and was dead, but the pig lived happily ever after.

LITTLE RED RIDING HOOD
Illustrated by Martin Aitchinson

Little Red Riding Hood set off one morning to visit her poor, sick Grandmamma. She carried a basket of sweet cakes and skipped happily along the forest path. Suddenly a big wolf stepped out from behind a tree and smiled at her. Now Little Red Riding Hood had never met a wolf before and so she was not afraid but the wicked wolf licked his lips and thought how nice it would be to eat this little girl all up.

"Where are you going?" asked the big, bad wolf.

"I am going to visit my Grandmamma," answered Little Red Riding Hood. "She lives in the cottage right in the middle of the wood."

"I will get there before her," thought the wolf to himself and off he ran. Soon he was peering inside the cottage window and there lay Grandmamma tucked up in bed. In two ticks the wolf was through the door and had eaten her up, spectacles and all! Then he tied her lace bonnet over his head, crawled into bed and pulled the blankets up under his chin.

Soon Little Red Riding Hood arrived at the cottage and she knocked upon the door.

"Pull the bobbin to lift the latch," called the wolf and he sounded very like Grandmamma.

But when the little girl sat down beside the bed she was astonished to see how peculiar her Grandmamma looked in her night-clothes.

"Oh, Grandmamma, what big ears you have!" said Little Red Riding Hood.

"All the better to hear you with!" replied the wolf.

"Oh, Grandmamma, what big eyes you have!"

"All the better to see you with!" replied the wolf.

"Oh, Grandmamma, what big teeth you have!"

"All the better to eat you with!" cried the wolf as he leapt from the bed and he gobbled down Little Red Riding Hood in one mouthful.

Now, a little while later a woodcutter was passing by and he decided to pay Grandmamma a visit.

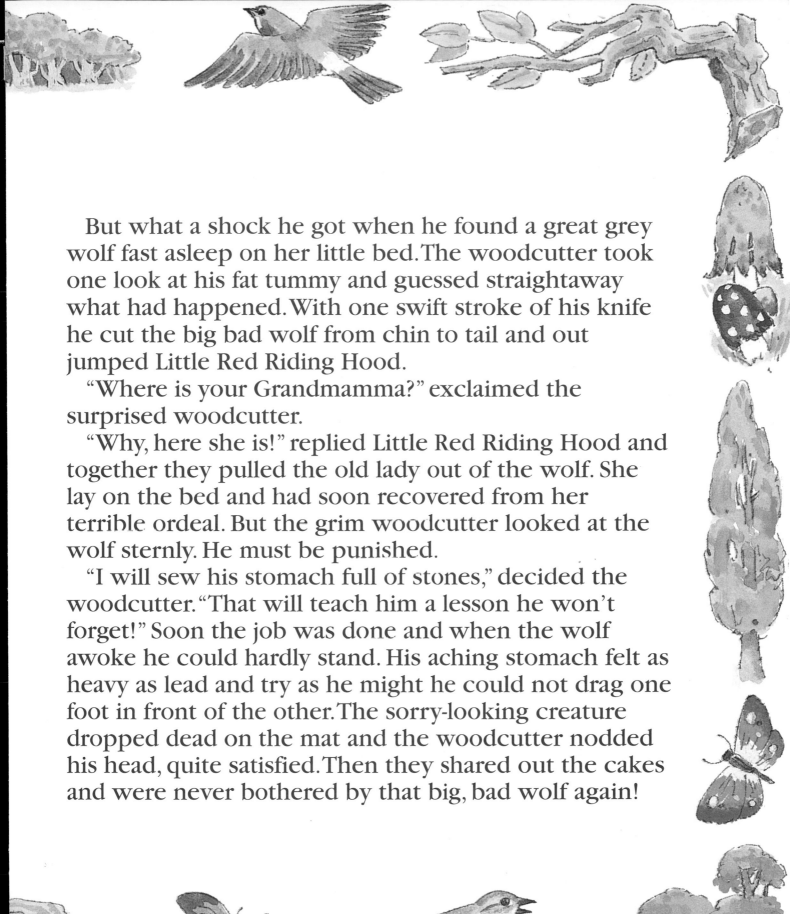

But what a shock he got when he found a great grey wolf fast asleep on her little bed. The woodcutter took one look at his fat tummy and guessed straightaway what had happened. With one swift stroke of his knife he cut the big bad wolf from chin to tail and out jumped Little Red Riding Hood.

"Where is your Grandmamma?" exclaimed the surprised woodcutter.

"Why, here she is!" replied Little Red Riding Hood and together they pulled the old lady out of the wolf. She lay on the bed and had soon recovered from her terrible ordeal. But the grim woodcutter looked at the wolf sternly. He must be punished.

"I will sew his stomach full of stones," decided the woodcutter. "That will teach him a lesson he won't forget!" Soon the job was done and when the wolf awoke he could hardly stand. His aching stomach felt as heavy as lead and try as he might he could not drag one foot in front of the other. The sorry-looking creature dropped dead on the mat and the woodcutter nodded his head, quite satisfied. Then they shared out the cakes and were never bothered by that big, bad wolf again!

THE THREE BILLY GOATS GRUFF
Illustrated by Martin Aitchinson

Once upon a time in a land far away there lived three Billy Goats. There was a large Billy Goat, a middle-sized Billy Goat and a small Billy Goat. They were the Three Billy Goats Gruff.

They lived high up on a rocky mountainside and leapt from peak to peak in search of food. But they found very little grass and often went to sleep with their empty tummies rumbling with hunger.

"We will look for a better place to live," decided the oldest Billy Goat at last. "Somewhere with plenty of good, sweet grass to eat."

Soon they had reached the valley far below.

"That is the place for us," said the oldest Billy Goat and he nodded his head at a lush green meadow on the other side of a swift mountain stream. Now the only way to cross that stream was over a rickety wooden bridge and under that rickety wooden bridge lived the ugliest, fiercest troll that ever was. He liked nothing better than to gobble up goats for his supper. But the smallest Billy Goat Gruff stamped his hoof and set off over the bridge, trip, trap, trip, trap.

"Who's that trip-trapping over my bridge?" roared the troll and the little Billy Goat stood stockstill.

"It is me, the smallest Billy Goat Gruff," he said. "I am off to the meadow to eat the sweet grass."

"Oh, no, you are not!" roared the troll, "for I am going to eat you all up!"

"But I am small and bony," replied the smallest Billy Goat. "You should wait for my brother. He is much fatter than me." The troll scratched his head and the smallest Billy Goat Gruff quickly trotted over the bridge and was soon safe on the other side. Then the middle-sized Billy Goat Gruff began to cross the bridge.

"Who is that trip-trapping over my bridge?" roared the ugly, fierce troll.

"It is me, the middle-sized Billy Goat Gruff and I am off to the meadow to eat the sweet grass," he said.

"Oh, no, you are not! I am going to gobble you up!" cried the troll and he reared up from his hiding place.

"You don't want to do that," replied the Billy Goat. "You should wait for my big brother."

So the troll let the middle-sized Billy Goat past and waited for the largest Billy Goat Gruff to pass by. Soon he came trotting over the bridge, trip, trap, trip, trap.

"Who is that trip-trapping over my bridge?" roared the angry troll. "I am going to eat you all up!" But the biggest Billy Goat Gruff did not look at all afraid. He pawed the rickety wooden bridge with his strong hooves, lowered his head and then the troll suddenly spotted his two sharp horns — but it was too late! The big Billy Goat Gruff thundered towards him and his mighty horns butted the troll high into the air. He landed in the river with a loud splash and was never seen again. And the Three Billy Goats Gruff lived happily ever after in their lush meadow and grew very fat indeed!

THE WIND IN THE WILLOWS:

THE RIVERBANK

❧

THE WILD WOOD

❧

THE ADVENTURES OF TOAD

❧

RETURN TO TOAD HALL

1 THE RIVERBANK

The Mole had been working very hard all the morning, spring-cleaning his little home and now he had dust in his throat and splashes of whitewash all over his black fur.

Spring was moving in the air above and in the earth below, entering even his dark and lowly little house with its spirit of change. It was small wonder then that the Mole suddenly flung down his brush and with a "Hang spring-cleaning!" bolted out of the house without even stopping to put on his coat.

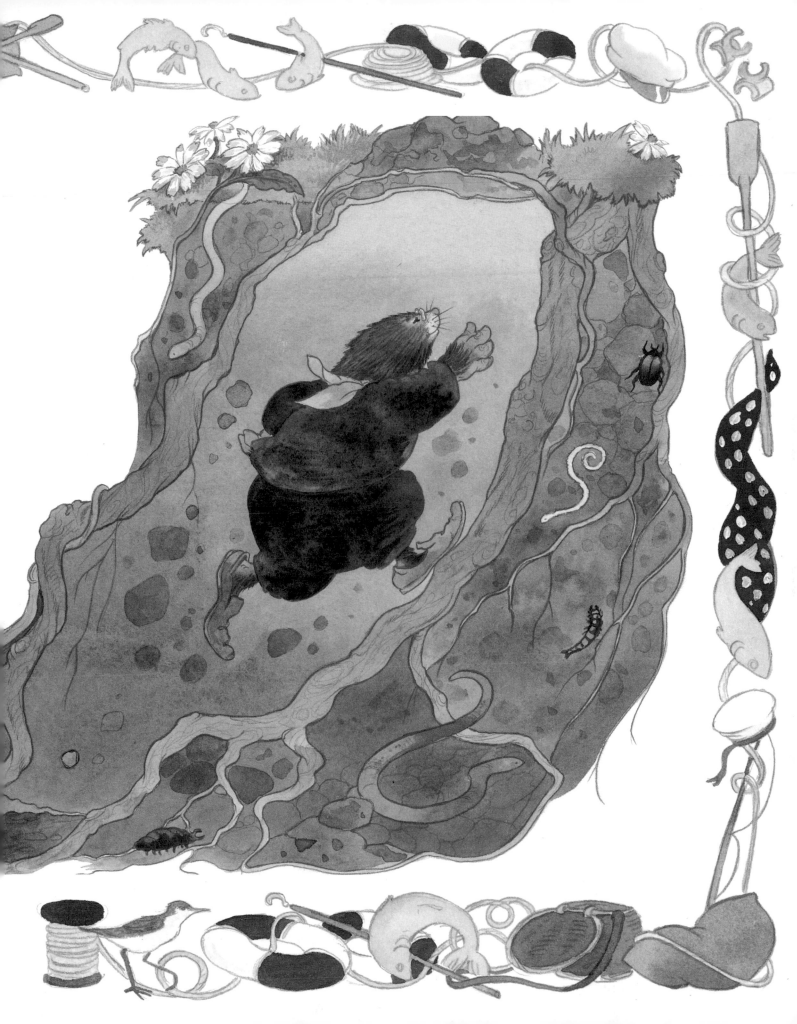

Something far off was calling him imperiously, and he scraped and scrabbled and scrooged his way up the steep little tunnel which led to the fresh air high above till at last, pop! his snout came out into the sunlight and he found himself rolling in the warm grass of a great meadow.

"This is fine!" he said to himself. "This is better than whitewashing!" and off he set across the field. Along the hedgerows he rambled, through the copses, finding everywhere birds building, flowers budding and leaves thrusting — everything happy and occupied. Suddenly he came to the edge of a full-fed river. Never in his life had he seen a river before — this sleek, sinuous-bodied animal, chasing and chuckling, grabbing things with a gurgle and leaving them with a laugh. All was a-shake and a-shiver — glints and gleams and sparkles, rustle and swirl, chatter and bubble.

As the delighted Mole gazed across to the other side he saw something bright and small seem to twinkle, then vanish. Soon he could make out that it was an eye — in a small brown face with whiskers.

It was none other than the Water Rat. The two animals regarded each other cautiously.

"Hullo, Mole!" said the Water Rat.

"Hullo, Rat!" said the Mole. Then the Rat stooped and unfastened a rope and to his great delight the Mole saw that it led to the nicest little blue boat.

"Would you like to come across?" asked the Rat and soon Mole found himself actually seated in the stern of a real boat.

"I have never been in a boat before in all my life," confessed the Mole shyly. Rat was astonished.

"Why," he said dreamily, "there is nothing — absolutely nothing — half so much worth doing as simply messing about in boats. Simply messing — messing — about — in — boats —"

"Look ahead!" cried the Mole, but it was too late!

Rat picked himself up with a laugh.

"Look here!" he said. "Suppose we drop down the river together and make a day of it?" The Mole waggled his toes from sheer happiness and leaned back blissfully on the soft cushions.

"Let us start at once!" he said. But first the Rat tied the boat up at the landing-stage, climbed into his hole, then reappeared with a fat, wicker basket.

"Shove that under your feet," he observed to Mole.

"What's inside it?" asked the Mole, curiously.

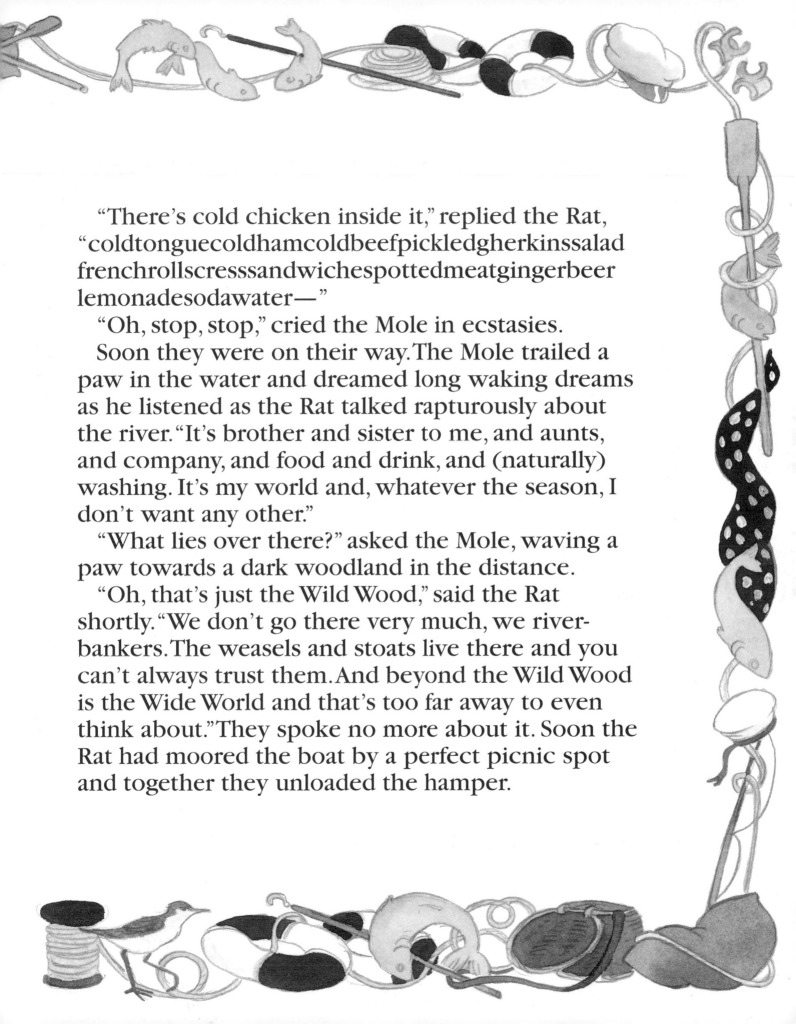

"There's cold chicken inside it," replied the Rat, "coldtonguecoldhamcoldbeefpickledgherkinssalad frenchrollscresssandwichespottedmeatgingerbeer lemonadesodawater—"

"Oh, stop, stop," cried the Mole in ecstasies.

Soon they were on their way. The Mole trailed a paw in the water and dreamed long waking dreams as he listened as the Rat talked rapturously about the river. "It's brother and sister to me, and aunts, and company, and food and drink, and (naturally) washing. It's my world and, whatever the season, I don't want any other."

"What lies over there?" asked the Mole, waving a paw towards a dark woodland in the distance.

"Oh, that's just the Wild Wood," said the Rat shortly. "We don't go there very much, we river-bankers. The weasels and stoats live there and you can't always trust them. And beyond the Wild Wood is the Wide World and that's too far away to even think about." They spoke no more about it. Soon the Rat had moored the boat by a perfect picnic spot and together they unloaded the hamper.

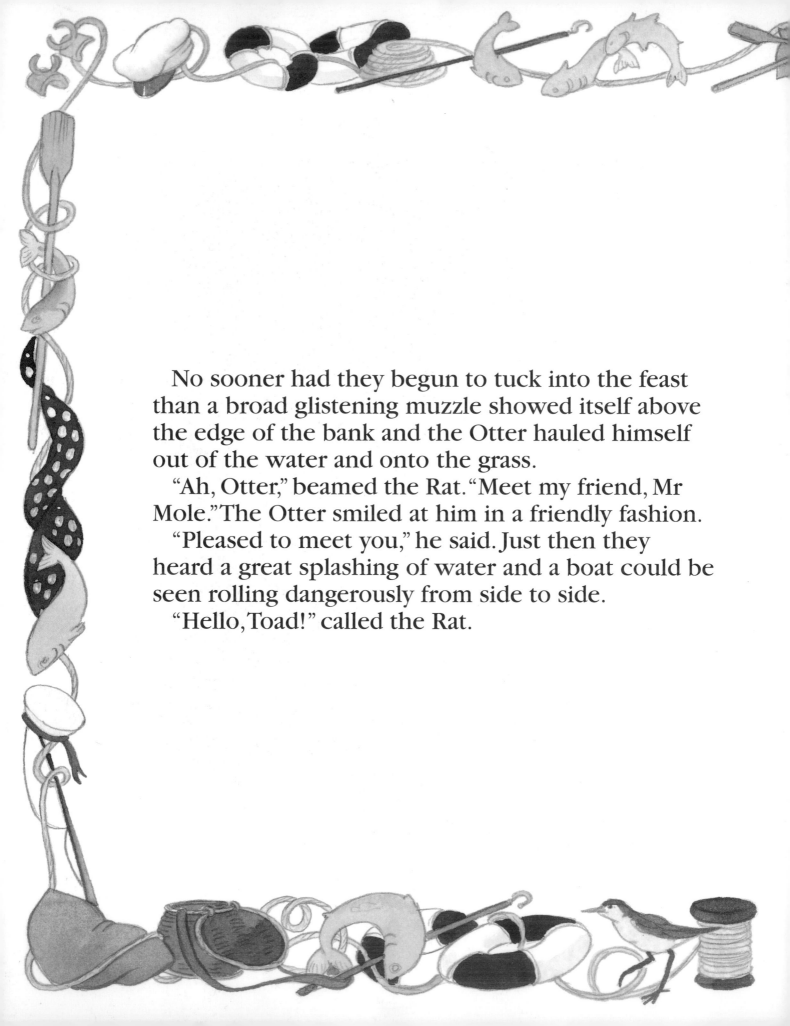

No sooner had they begun to tuck into the feast than a broad glistening muzzle showed itself above the edge of the bank and the Otter hauled himself out of the water and onto the grass.

"Ah, Otter," beamed the Rat. "Meet my friend, Mr Mole." The Otter smiled at him in a friendly fashion.

"Pleased to meet you," he said. Just then they heard a great splashing of water and a boat could be seen rolling dangerously from side to side.

"Hello, Toad!" called the Rat.

The Mole was delighted to make the acquaintance of such an important figure as Mr Toad but all too soon the sun began to sink in the sky and, after carefully packing the hamper, Rat and Mole headed back up the river. The Mole watched Rat sculling along strongly and he wished he could try it himself.

"Oh, no. It is not as easy as it looks," said the Rat with a shake of his head. But the Mole was determined and he suddenly jumped up and seized the sculls. In a trice the whole boat was over!

Oh, how cold the water was, and how wet! But
the Rat fished Mole out in next to no time and soon
had him running up and down the towpath to
warm up. The hamper was retrieved from the river
bed and they set off once again for Rat's cosy home.

"Don't worry," Rat told the ashamed Mole. "I will
teach you how to row and soon you'll be as handy
on the water as any of us." The Mole was so touched
by his kindness that he could hardly speak.

At last they were indoors in front of a roaring fire
and the tired Mole lay back in Rat's comfiest chair in
peace and great contentment. What a day he had had!

2 THE WILD WOOD

As the months passed by, the Mole and the Rat became the best of friends. But there was one person who the curious Mole longed to meet and that was the Badger who lived in the middle of the Wild Wood. One wintery day Mole set off to find him, leaving the Rat dozing in front of his fire. But as Mole entered the wood, the light seemed to drain away and he suddenly began to see small spiteful faces peeking out from behind the trees.

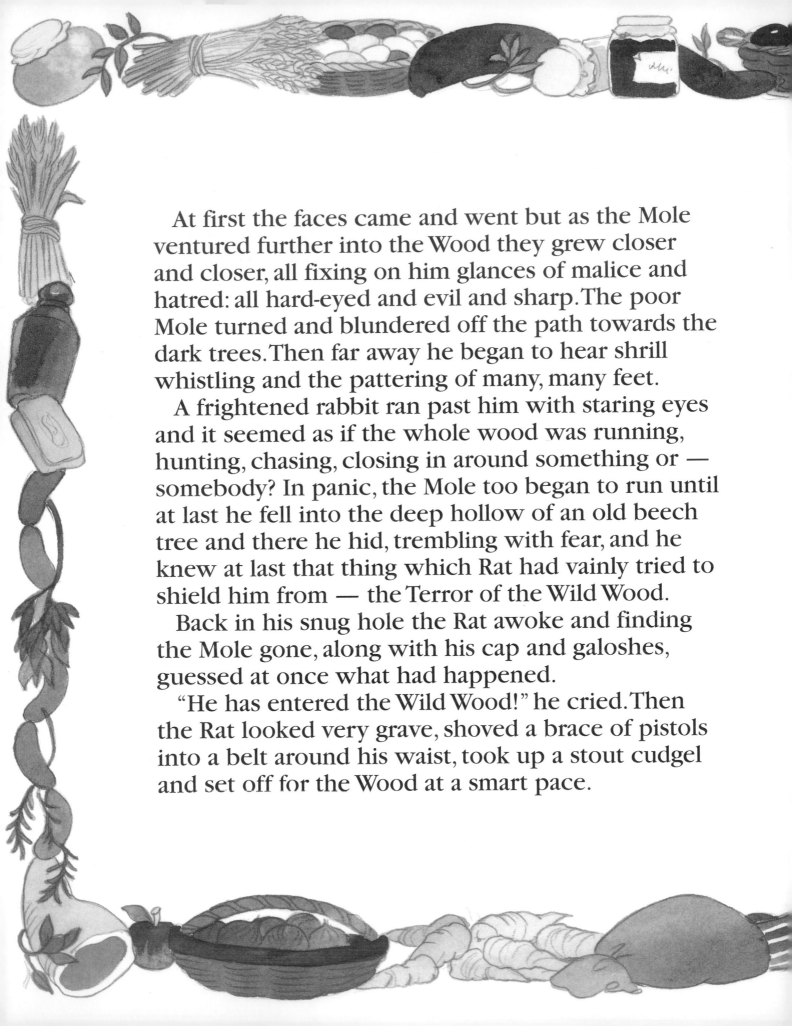

At first the faces came and went but as the Mole ventured further into the Wood they grew closer and closer, all fixing on him glances of malice and hatred: all hard-eyed and evil and sharp. The poor Mole turned and blundered off the path towards the dark trees. Then far away he began to hear shrill whistling and the pattering of many, many feet.

A frightened rabbit ran past him with staring eyes and it seemed as if the whole wood was running, hunting, chasing, closing in around something or — somebody? In panic, the Mole too began to run until at last he fell into the deep hollow of an old beech tree and there he hid, trembling with fear, and he knew at last that thing which Rat had vainly tried to shield him from — the Terror of the Wild Wood.

Back in his snug hole the Rat awoke and finding the Mole gone, along with his cap and galoshes, guessed at once what had happened.

"He has entered the Wild Wood!" he cried. Then the Rat looked very grave, shoved a brace of pistols into a belt around his waist, took up a stout cudgel and set off for the Wood at a smart pace.

It was nearly dusk when he plunged between the trees and began to search for his friend. Here and there wicked little faces popped out of holes but vanished immediately at the sight of the brave animal, his pistols and the stout cudgel.

"Moly, Moly, Moly!" cried the Rat. "Where are you?" After an hour or more he heard a little answering cry and there in the dark hollow of the tree he found the Mole, still trembling with fear.

Night had fallen and the poor animal begged to be allowed to take a nap before returning for home. But when at last he awoke and they looked outside, they found that a heavy snow had fallen on the Wood!

Through the heavy drifts they trudged for hours, hardly knowing where they were going, until at last the Mole tripped up and fell on his face with a squeal.

"That's funny!" said the Rat. "Something hard and sharp is under here." Soon they were both busy scraping away at the snow and then the Rat gave a delighted whoop of joy.

"It is a door-scraper — and here is the door!"

"It's Badger's home! Pull that bell-rope, Moly!" cried the Rat, and soon they could hear the Badger's shuffling footsteps approaching.

"Why, Ratty, my dear little man!" exclaimed the Badger. "Come along in, with your little friend. Well I never! Lost in the snow! And in the Wild Wood, too!"

Soon they were tucked up in dressing-gowns on the settee next to the fire while Badger bathed Mole's cut and after a while it seemed as if all that they had suffered was a half-forgotten dream. The Mole was thrilled to meet the Badger at long last and found him just as the Rat had described him, the very kindest of animals. "Come and eat!" urged the Badger, "and in between mouthfuls you must tell me all about the news in your part of the world. How is old Toad?"

As the Mole and Rat tucked in with gusto, they told the Badger all about Toad's new passion.

"He has lost interest in everything apart from motor cars," said the Rat with a shake of his head.

"He's been in hospital three times," added the Mole, "and had terrible fines to pay for dangerous driving!"

The Badger looked severe. "Well, of course I can't do anything now in the middle of winter, you understand, but come the spring, well, then we'll take Toad seriously in hand." The Rat yawned and soon they were tucked up in the softest of little white beds and there they slept until late the next day.

As the Rat and the Mole tucked into a hearty breakfast, the Otter came bounding into the room.

"We've all been out looking for you!" he cried, "but I thought I should find you here!" and he gave the Rat a big hug. The sight of this friendly water animal made the Rat realise how much he missed his river bank.

"Come on, Mole," he said. "Badger has been very kind but it's high time we left him in peace." The Badger led them through a secret tunnel under the wood and soon they found themselves on the edge of the fields. Looking back they saw the whole mass of the Wild Wood, dense and menacing, then together they turned away and headed for home.

3 THE ADVENTURES OF TOAD

The winter passed slowly but at long last spring arrived. The Mole and the Water Rat were just finishing their breakfast when in strode the Badger. "The hour has come!" he announced solemnly. "I have just heard that another new motor-car has been delivered to Toad Hall. It is time for us to take Toad in hand!" Soon the three of them were marching up the drive to Toad Hall. There stood the car — and there stood the proud Toad!

"Take the wretched creature inside," ordered the Badger, "while I explain to the driver that Mr Toad will no longer be needing this vehicle."

Toad was furious! The Mole and the Rat pulled off his driving clothes and soon he was locked in his bedroom. "It's for your own good, Toady," said the Rat kindly. "Soon you will see sense and thank us for it."

But Toad did not thank them. He knotted his bedsheets together, climbed out of his window and was soon marching briskly on his way.

After a while Toad reached a little town and there standing outside The Red Lion Hotel was the most beautiful green car. Toad was in raptures!

Next moment, hardly knowing how it came about, he found himself sitting in the driver's seat. As if in a dream he pulled the lever and swung the car onto the high road. As he tore through open countryside he shouted aloud for joy. "Make way! Make way for Toad, the Terror of the Road!"

But once again, as had happened so many times before, Toad was apprehended by a large and burly policeman and before the day was out he found himself in court. This time the stern Judge was determined to punish him severely.

"You stole a motor-car. You drove dangerously, and, worst of all, you were appallingly rude to the rural policeman. In consequence of this I sentence you to twenty years in gaol!" Then the brutal minions of the law fell upon the hapless Toad and dragged him from the Court House, across the drawbridge, past guardrooms and sentries until they reached the grimmest dungeon deep in the innermost keep in the very heart of the stoutest castle in all the length and breadth of merry England.

As the brutish gaoler turned the key Toad flung himself upon the floor and shed bitter tears.

"O wise old Badger! O clever Rat and sensible Mole! How right you were!" he sobbed.

Now the gaoler had a daughter, a good-hearted girl, and she grew very fond of poor Toad. One day she made up her mind to help him.

"I have a plan," she told him. "My aunt is a washerwoman and she does all the washing for the prisoners. You and she are alike in many respects — particularly about the figure — so if you dress up in her clothes you could easily escape from the castle."

Toad thought this an excellent idea and in exchange for two gold sovereigns he received an old gown, an apron, a shawl and a black bonnet. At first the old lady hooted with laughter at the sight of Toad in her clothes but she soon stopped when she was bound and gagged in order to convince the gaoler that Toad had overcome her.

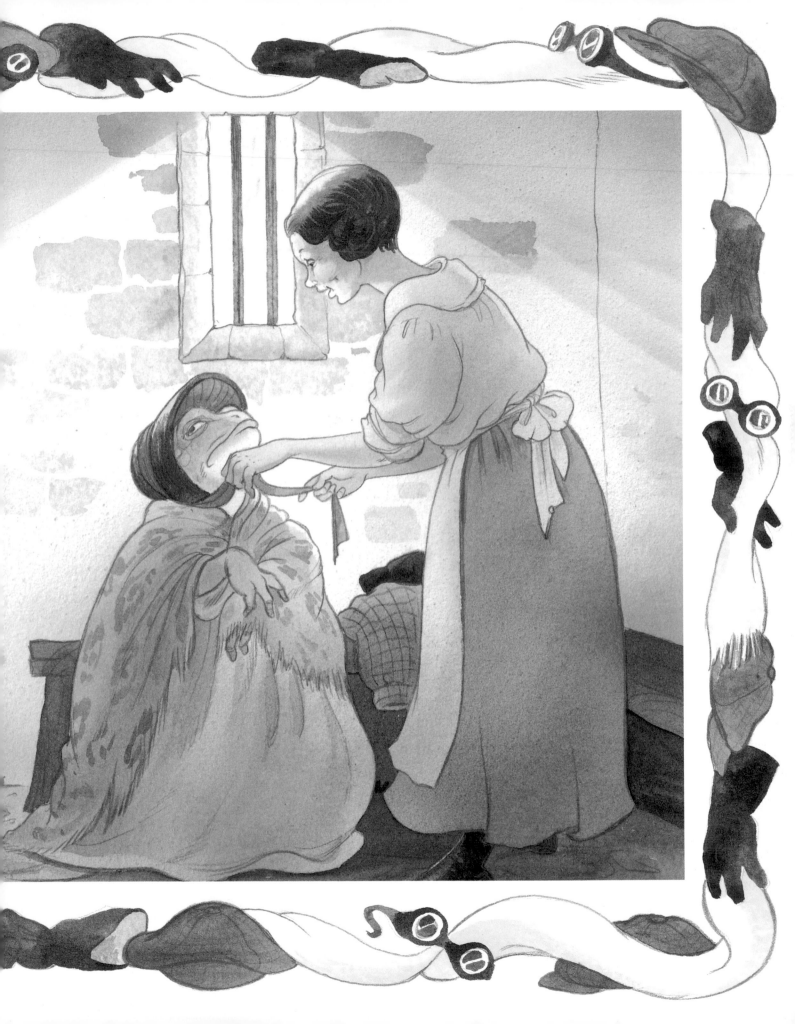

With a quaking heart, Toad set forth but he was agreeably surprised to find that everyone he met was entirely convinced that he was indeed the washerwoman. Soon he was shutting the last door behind him. Free at last! He walked quickly towards the railway station but when he tried to buy a ticket at the booking-office he realised to his horror that he had no money on him. It was in his waistcoat back in the dungeon! Full of despair the poor Toad wandered down the platform to where the train was standing, and tears trickled down his nose.

The engine-driver caught sight of Toad and felt sorry for him. "What's the trouble, mother?" he asked.

"O sir!" cried Toad. "I am a poor washerwoman and I've lost my money, and I can't get home!" Well, the engine-driver was a good-hearted fellow and soon he had invited Toad to join him in the cab.

"You ride along with me," he said, but as soon as they left the station and were steaming along the track, the driver leaned out of his cab and looked puzzled. "There's another train close behind us," he said "and it looks as if it's chasing us!"

Then Toad fell to his knees among the coals.

"Save me, save me, dear Mr Engine-driver," he begged. "I am not a washerwoman. I am the brave and popular Mr Toad and I have just escaped from a loathsome dungeon. I only borrowed a motor-car. I didn't mean to steal it! Do not let them catch me again!" The engine-driver looked very grave.

"I fear that you have indeed been a wicked Toad," he said, "but I'll help you if I can. There is a long tunnel up ahead. As we come out of the other end I will slow down and you must jump off and hide in the wood. Get ready!" So Toad gathered up his skirts, jumped down the bank, scrambled into the wood and hid. The train shot by full of policemen waving their truncheons and the happy Toad laughed and laughed. Then he dusted himself off and set forth. It wasn't long before he came upon a canal and there he found a horse pulling a barge.

"Good morning, ma'am," called Toad to the stout woman at the tiller. "I am a poor washerwoman trying to make my way home. Could you give me a lift?" Soon Toad found himself safely on board.

"What a bit of luck, meeting you!" observed the barge-woman. "I have a whole heap of things to be washed. You can scrub my clothes while I steer the barge." Well, poor Toad had never washed a thing in his life and the barge-woman laughed aloud to see the dreadful mess he made of it.

"How dare you laugh at me!" shouted Toad. "I will have you know that I am the very well-known and distinguished Toad!" The barge-woman wrinkled her nose in disgust. "I will have no Toads on *my* barge!" she exclaimed and, catching him by the leg, she threw him overboard.

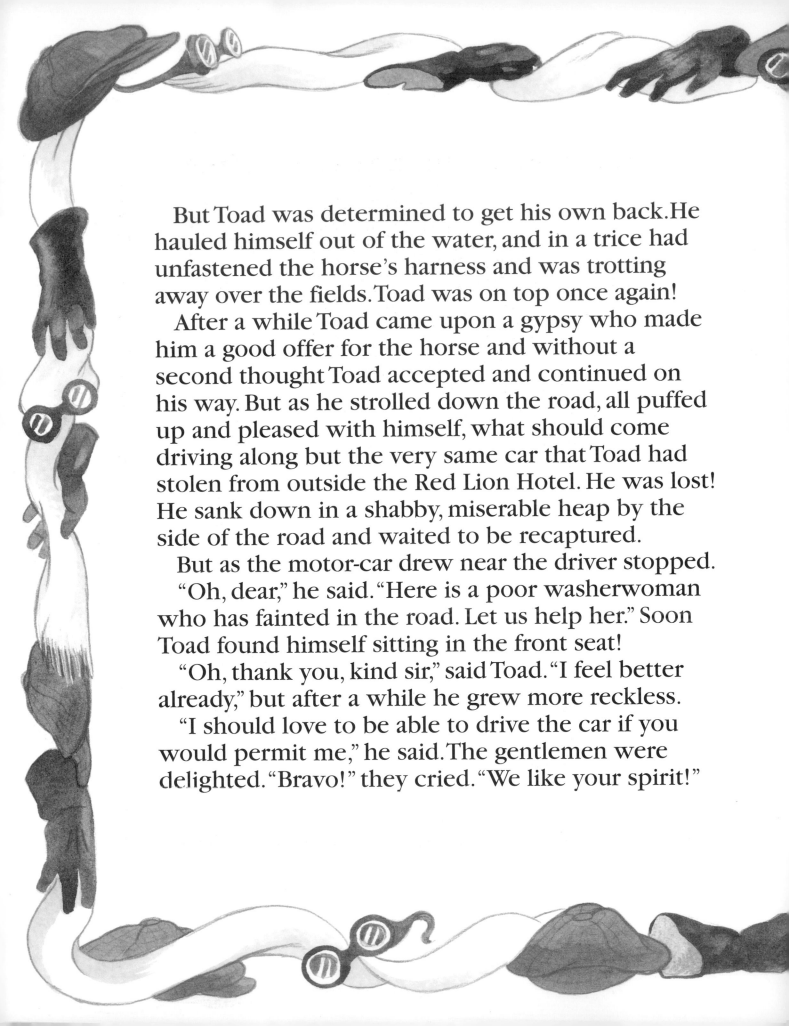

But Toad was determined to get his own back. He hauled himself out of the water, and in a trice had unfastened the horse's harness and was trotting away over the fields. Toad was on top once again!

After a while Toad came upon a gypsy who made him a good offer for the horse and without a second thought Toad accepted and continued on his way. But as he strolled down the road, all puffed up and pleased with himself, what should come driving along but the very same car that Toad had stolen from outside the Red Lion Hotel. He was lost! He sank down in a shabby, miserable heap by the side of the road and waited to be recaptured.

But as the motor-car drew near the driver stopped.

"Oh, dear," he said. "Here is a poor washerwoman who has fainted in the road. Let us help her." Soon Toad found himself sitting in the front seat!

"Oh, thank you, kind sir," said Toad. "I feel better already," but after a while he grew more reckless.

"I should love to be able to drive the car if you would permit me," he said. The gentlemen were delighted. "Bravo!" they cried. "We like your spirit!"

So it was that Toad found himself once more behind the wheel and then he began to lose his head.

"Ho, ho! I am the Toad," he cried. "The famous, the skilful, the entirely fearless Toad!" The horrified men flung themselves upon him and in a trice the car had crashed through a hedge and landed in a ditch.

Then Toad was off and running across country as hard as he could. He looked over his shoulder to where the men were hot on his trail and suddenly, splash! he found himself head over ears in deep, rapid water. He was swept along in the strong current until at last he managed to reach out and catch hold of a small hole in the bank. There he clung and after a while, to his great astonishment, a small brown face appeared. It was the Water Rat!

4 RETURN TO TOAD HALL

The Rat gripped the spluttering, waterlogged Toad by the scruff of the neck and pulled him inside. "Oh, Ratty!" cried Toad. "I've been through such times since I saw you last. Such sufferings!" But he got no sympathy at all from the exasperated Rat.

"Toad," he said sternly, "cars have brought you nothing but trouble. It grieves me to tell you that while you have been gallivanting all over the countryside the Wild Wooders have taken over Toad Hall!"

Then Rat told poor Toad the whole sorry tale.
"When the weasels and the stoats heard what had
happened to you, they got very cocky. One dark
night they armed themselves and broke into the
Hall and they have been living there ever since." The
tears welled up in Toad's eyes and fell to the floor.

"We must talk to the Mole and Badger," declared
the Rat, and so that evening they all met up.

"It's no good," sighed the Mole. "There are sentries
and guns everywhere. We could never get in."

Then the Badger coughed. "I have a secret," he
said. "I know of an underground passage which will
take us up right into the middle of Toad Hall!"

"We shall creep out —," cried the Mole.

"— with our pistols and sticks —," added the Rat.

"— and whack 'em hard!" cried the Toad joyfully.
Now the very next day the Wild Wooders were
going to have a party in Toad Hall and so, as the
sounds of shouting and cheering rang far above
them, the Brave Four crept along the secret tunnel.
Soon they were under a trapdoor in the kitchen.

"The hour is come!" shouted the Badger.

Into the room they rushed and what a squealing and squeaking and screeching filled the air! Terrified weasels dived under the tables and sprang madly up at the windows and frightened ferrets rushed wildly for the fireplace as the four Heroes strode up and down, their stout cudgels whistling through the air. The Wild Wooders fled with squeals of dismay and soon the battle for Toad Hall was over.

A great banquet was held in celebration of the victory and although Toad would very much have liked to fill the evening with his own speeches and songs, his friends persuaded him to reconsider and so the evening was judged a great success.

Indeed Toad seemed to turn over a new leaf and in time forgot his passion for cars altogether. On long summer evenings the four friends would stroll happily in the Wild Wood and it was pleasing to see how respectfully they were now greeted by the humble inhabitants. All was well once again!